BUMPER

Quiz Book

Derek O'Brien was born in Kolkata. He began his career as a journalist for *Sportsworld* magazine but soon shifted to advertising. After working for a number of very successful years as Creative Head of Ogilvy, Derek decided to focus all his energy and talent in his passion – quizzing.

Today, Derek is Asia's best-known quizmaster and the CEO of Derek O'Brien & Associates. He is the host of the longest-running game show on Indian television, the Cadbury Bournvita Quiz Contest, for which he was voted the Best Anchor of a Game Show at the Indian Television Academy Awards for three years in a row. Always innovating, Derek is also credited with having conducted the first quiz on Twitter in 2010.

Derek has written over fifty bestselling reference, quiz and textbooks. In 2011, he was voted to the Rajya Sabha as a Member of Parliament (MP) and is the Leader of the Trinamool Congress Parliamentary Party in the Rajya Sabha.

Keep in touch with Derek on Twitter, where his

Other books by Derek O'Brien
(published by Rupa Publications)

Bournvita Quiz Contest Quiz Book 2012

The Ultimate BQC Book of Knowledge (Volumes 1 and 2)

The Best of BQC

Derek's Challenge

Speak Up, Speak Out: My Favourite Elocution Pieces and How to Deliver Them

My Way: Success Mantras of 12 Achievers

Derek Introduces: 100 Iconic Indians

Bournvita Quiz Contest Quiz Book 2014

BQC Quiz Book 3

BUMPER

Quiz Book

DEREK O'BRIEN

RUPA

Published by
Rupa Publications India Pvt. Ltd 2016
7/16, Ansari Road, Daryaganj
New Delhi 110002

Sales Centres:
Allahabad Bengaluru Chennai
Hyderabad Jaipur Kathmandu
Kolkata Mumbai

Copyright © Derek O'Brien & Associates 2016

'Cadbury' and 'Bournvita' are registered trademarks of
Cadbury India Limited.

The views and opinions expressed in this book are the author's own and
the facts are as reported by him/her which have been verified to the extent possible, and the publishers are not in any way liable for the same.

All rights reserved.
No part of this publication may be reproduced, stored in a retrieval
system, or transmitted, in any form or by any means, electronic,
mechanical, photocopying, recording or otherwise, without the prior
permission of the publishers.

ISBN: 978-81-291-4041-8

Sixth impression 2018

10 9 8 7 6

The moral right of the author has been asserted.

This book is sold subject to the condition that it shall not,
by way of trade or otherwise, be lent, resold, hired out, or otherwise
circulated, without the publisher's prior consent, in any form of binding or
cover other than that in which it is published.

HALL OF FAME

PAST WINNERS OF THE BOURNVITA QUIZ CONTEST

1994-1995, Mumbai

Campion High School, Mumbai
Balakrishnan Sivaraman, Sudhanshu Bhuwalka

1995-1996, Mumbai

Kendriya Vidyalaya, Powai, Mumbai
Eipy Koshy, Gourav Shah

1996-1997, Mumbai

Bombay International High School, Mumbai
Nirica Borges, Advait Behara

1997, Mumbai

Mount Saint Mary's School, New Delhi
Joe Christy, Maninder Singh Jessel

1997-1998, Mumbai

Bombay Scottish High School, Mumbai
Shaambhavi Pandyaa, Rahul Lalmalani

1998, Mumbai

Sacred Heart Convent School, Jamshedpur
Ela Verma, Lavanya Raghavan

1998-1999, Mumbai
Indian School Al Ghubra, Muscat
Anand Raghavan, Hitesh Kanvatirtha

1999, Mumbai
Maneckji Cooper High School, Mumbai
Ipsita Bandopadhyay, Gourav Bhattacharya

1999-2000, Mumbai
Chettinad Vidyashram, Chennai
Siddharth, Karthik Das

2000-2001, Mumbai
Bharatiya Vidya Bhavan, Hyderabad
Ananya Bhaskar, Aksha Anand

2001 September, Mumbai
Brightlands, Dehradun
Ankur Bharadwaj, Shray Sharma

2001 December, Mumbai
Little Flower High School, Hyderabad
G. Mithilesh, K Siddharth Reddy

2002 February, Bentota, Sri Lanka
G.D. Birla Centre For Education, Kolkata
Namrata Basu, Rituparna Dey

2002 June, Mumbai
Kerala Samajam Public School, Jamshedpur
Saurav Biswas, Kunal Mohan

2002 September, Mumbai
Jamnabai Narsee School, Mumbai
Sharan Narayanan, Vishnu Shrest

2003 January, Kerala
Naval Public High School, Mumbai
Apoorva Sharma, Abhishek Pandit

2003 May, Kolkata
St. Patrick's Higher Secondary School, Asansol
Pushpen Dasgupta, Shamik Ray

2003 October, Sangla
St. Agnes Loreto Day School, Lucknow
Aastha Srivastava, Illa Gupta

2004 February, Swabhumi, Kolkata
Apeejay School, Jalandhar
Mohit Thukral, Sahil Sareen

2004 May, Goa
Springdales School, Delhi
Anirudh Sridhar, B. Anuraag

2004 July, Indian Military Academy, Dehradun
The Mother's International School, Delhi
Krittika Adhikary, Milind Ganjoo

2004 November, Kolkata
Amity International, New Delhi
Aishwarya Singhal, Adarsh Modi

2005 August, Kolkata
Amity International, New Delhi
Utkarsh Johari/ Aishwarya Singhal

2006 July, Kolkata
Riverdale High School, Dehradun
Kartikeya Panwar/ Sumit Nair

2006 November, Kolkata
Seth Jaipuria School, Lucknow
Ratnaksha Lele/ Ananya Kumar Singh

2011 August, Kolkata
Amity International School, Noida
Kripi Badonia/ Shinjini Biswas

2012 January, Kolkata
Birla Vidya Niketan, New Delhi
Anusha Malhotra/ Nitya Bansal

2013 January, Kolkata
Vidyaniketan Public School(Ullal), Bengaluru
Shashank Niranjan Gowda, Mainak Mandal

2014 December, Kolkata
Centre Point, Amravati Road, Nagpur
Ratnasambhav Sahu/Tanaya Ramani

SET 1

TAKE YOUR PICK

1. 'Learn from yesterday, live for today, hope for tomorrow. The important thing is not to stop _____.' Fill in the blank to complete this quotation by Albert Einstein.
   a. Wishing
   b. Questioning
   c. Thinking

2. The name of which spice comes from the French word for 'nail'?
   a. Cinnamon
   b. Cardamom
   c. Clove

3. In India, the train Lifeline Express is a…
   a. Hospital
   b. Bank
   c. Primary School

4. Which Asian mountain is also known as the Savage Mountain due to the extreme difficulty of ascent?
   a. Kanchenjunga
   b. K2
   c. Lhotse

5. In 1964, which portfolio was given to Indira Gandhi in the government of Lal Bahadur Shastri?
   a. Defence
   b. Home
   c. Information and Broadcasting

6. In *Alice's Adventures in Wonderland*, which game was played by the Queen of Hearts using hedgehogs as balls?
   a. Quintet
   b. Quidditch
   c. Croquet

7. With which unfortunate incident would you associate the warplane Enola Gay?
   a. Sinking of the ship Bismark
   b. The Hiroshima bombing
   c. Storming of Bastille

8. Odhra Magadha is the precursor to which Indian dance form?
   a. Kuchipudi
   b. Kathak
   c. Odissi

9. Who composed music for the 1969 film *Goopy Gyne Bagha Byne*?
   a. Satyajit Ray
   b. Ravi Shankar
   c. Shiv-Hari

10. Where in the human body is the stapedius muscle situated?
    a. Nose
    b. Ears
    c. Leg

WHAT'S THE QUESTION

1. She lives in St Mary Mead.
2. Kleptomaniac
3. The first batsman to score 10,000 runs in Test crickct.
4. Albumen
5. Ranko the gorilla appeared in this Tintin adventure.
6. It is called a drey.
7. Isohyet
8. Silk Route
9. The Heartbreak Kid
10. Epitaph

MIXED BAG

1. The name of which primate, found only in Madagascar, comes from a Latin word meaning 'spirits of the dead'?
2. Who is the only US president to be awarded the Pulitzer Prize?
3. What does Mysore Paints and Varnishes Limited provide during an election?
4. What is the Pygmallion Point, the extreme southern point of Great Nicobar, now called?
5. Which famous Indian cricketer starred in the 1980

film *Savli Premachi*?
6. Which author's collection of short stories, titled *Soz-e-Watan*, in Urdu was banned by the British?
7. Which is the hardest naturally occurring substance known?
8. Which leader, born in Braunau am Inn, twice failed to secure entry to the Academy of Fine Arts?
9. What is a rockumentary?
10. Tussar, Muga and Endi are varieties of what?

SPOT THE ANSWER

1. What is a pollywog?
    a. A cute golliwog
    b. A green parrot
    c. A tadpole
2. The first session of which of these was held at the Gokuldas Tejpal Sanskrit College?
    a. The Association of Quiz Organizers
    b. The Red Cross in India
    c. The Indian National Congress
3. Sansarpur, often known as the Mecca of Hockey, is located in which state of India?
    a. Punjab
    b. West Bengal
    c. Bihar
4. The construction of which tower started in 1173 AD on a piece of land known as Piazza dei Miracoli?
    a. White House
    b. Eiffel Tower
    c. Leaning Tower of Pisa

5. In the book *The Adventures of Tom Sawyer*, how does the villian, Injun Joe, die?
   a. He is trapped in a cave and dies of starvation.
   b. He drowns in a lake.
   c. A chicken bone gets stuck in his throat.

CONFIDENCE ROUND

1. Which fruit is 'Dussehri' a variety of?
2. How many zeroes are there in 10 crore (100 million)?
3. What do even bald men wear to keep out the sun: caps or cravats?
4. Calcium oxide is another name for quicklime or quicksilver?
5. All leopards have spots: serious or joking?
6. What was Aristotle's nationality?
7. If Juhu beach is in Maharashtra, where is Chowpatty?
8. Which gland swells to a goitre?
9. Who is India's first Formula 1 driver?
10. Which desert fills nearly all of northern Africa?

WHAT'S THE WORD

Set 1

1. Mandolin is a stringed instrument. Serious or Joking?
2. Spaghetti, macaroni and ravioli are varieties of pasta or cheese?
3. In 2004, against which team did Brian Lara score 400 runs in a single Test innings: England or India?
4. Who wrote *The Praise of Folly*: Erasmus or Socrates?

5. Which element forms more compounds than all the other elements combined?
6. Of which small bird are giant, bee and ruby-throated species?
7. What is the word?

Set 2

1. Who is well known for his treatise on geometry called the *Elements*: Euclid or Plato?
2. In Hindu mythology, who was Nakula's mother: Madri or Draupadi?
3. The Louvre Museum is in which capital city: Paris or London?
4. In which country would you be if you land at Baghdad International Airport?
5. Burgundy is dark red or green?
6. What is the strong black coffee, which is made by forcing steam through the ground coffee beans called?
7. What is the word?

Set 3

1. Who was the famous father of Amitabh Bachchan?
2. The name of which continent means 'opposite to the Arctic'?
3. What is the official office of the president of the United States called: Pink House or White House?
4. Which NASA astronaut graduated from Tagore School, Karnal, India, in 1976?
5. *Mammuthus* is the extinct genus of which present-day animal?
6. Which literary character's companion was Friday?

7. What is the word?

Set 4

1. Who played Chandramukhi in Sanjay Leela Bhansali's *Devdas*?
2. In 1985, which team did Sri Lanka defeat to register its first-ever win in ODIs: India or Zimbabwe?
3. What is the capital of Assam?
4. Which word connects a dark brown oval fruit and a number specifying a day?
5. What does 'L' in LASER stand for?
6. Ocular albinism is a genetic condition that primarily affects which organ of the body?
7. What is the word?

Set 5

1. Who was the founder of the Mauryan dynasty: Chandragupta or Brihadratha?
2. Of which fruit are blood, navel and sour varieties: oranges or grapes?
3. In Hindu mythology, Swaha is the wife of which god: Agni or Indra?
4. Vasundhara Raje was the first woman chief minister of which state?
5. With which instrument was Pandit Ravi Shankar associated?
6. Which flightless bird is the second largest living bird?
7. What is the word?

MATHS AND IQ

1. Which number should logically replace the question mark?
   7   49   343   ?

2. Fill in the blanks with either addition, subtraction, multiplication or division to figure out the correct answer. Go sequentially from left to right without following BODMAS.

   | 30 | | 15 | | 4 | | 1 | = | 5 |

3. If CRANE=RAN, then SPODE =?

4. Insert the missing number:
   196   (25) 324
   329   ( ) 137

5. Fill in the blanks with either addition, subtraction, multiplication or division to figure out the correct answer. Go sequentially from left to right without following BODMAS.

   | 60 | | 24 | | 14 | | 10 | = | 7 |

VOCABULARY

1. Rearrange the letters of the word 'MADE' to get the feminine version of Sir.
2. Rearrange the letters of the word 'LOUSE' to get the name of a Korean city.

3. Rearrange the letters of the word 'MASTER' to get a flowing water body.
4. Read the word 'MART' backwards to get a means of transport.
5. Read the word 'LAID' backwards to get what you do on the telephone.

SPEED

1. What does a Giant Panda's diet mainly consist of?
2. The Statue of Liberty wears a cap, a crown or a garland?
3. How many yolks will one dozen perfect chicken eggs produce?
4. The Simla Agreement of 1972 was signed between India and which other country?
5. Who was the first scientist to describe the laws of motion?
6. Which film maker received an Honorary Oscar for Lifetime Achievement in 1992?
7. Do swimmers float more easily in a swimming pool or in the sea?
8. Which river in Africa means 'Great River' in the language of the Tonga people?
9. Who became the first Indian woman to win an Olympic medal at the 2000 Sydney Olympics?
10. What are the sharp thin leaves of a fir or pine tree called: needles or nails?

ANSWERS

TAKE YOUR PICK

1. Questioning
2. Clove
3. Hospital
4. K2
5. Information and Broadcasting
6. Croquet
7. The Hiroshima bombing
8. Odissi
9. Satyajit Ray
10. Ears

WHAT'S THE QUESTION

1. Where does Miss Marple live?
2. Which word describes a person with a recurrent urge for stealing things?
3. Who is Sunil Gavaskar?
4. What is the white portion of an egg called?
5. What is The Black Island?
6. What do we call a squirrel's nest?
7. What do you call the lines on a map that connect places receiving the same amount of rainfall in a given period?
8. What is the name of the ancient trade route between China and the West?

9. In the World Wrestling Federation, what is Shawn Michaels' nickname?
10. What do you call the words written on a tombstone?

MIXED BAG

1. Lemur
2. John F. Kennedy
3. Indelible ink
4. India Point
5. Sunil Gavaskar
6. Premchand
7. Diamond
8. Adolf Hitler
9. A documentary on rockstars and rock music.
10. Silk

SPOT THE ANSWER

1. A tadpole. The tadpole is the aquatic larval stage of an amphibian.
2. The Indian National Congress. It was founded on 28 December 1885, and played a major role in India's freedom struggle.
3. Punjab
4. Leaning Tower of Pisa
5. He is trapped in a cave and dies of starvation.

CONFIDENCE ROUND

1. Mango

2. Eight
3. Caps
4. Quicklime
5. Serious
6. Greek
7. Also in Maharashtra. Both are located in Mumbai.
8. The thyroid gland
9. Narain Karthikeyan
10. Sahara

WHAT'S THE WORD

Set 1
1. Serious
2. Pasta
3. England
4. Erasmus
5. Carbon
6. Hummingbird
7. SPEECH

Set 2
1. Euclid
2. Madri
3. Paris
4. Iraq
5. Red
6. Espresso
7. EMPIRE

Set 3

1. Harivanshrai Bachchan
2. Antarctica
3. White House
4. Kalpana Chawla
5. Elephant
6. Robinson Crusoe
7. HAWKER

Set 4

1. Madhuri Dixit
2. India
3. Dispur
4. Date
5. Light
6. Eyes
7. MIDDLE

Set 5

1. Chandragupta Maurya
2. Oranges
3. Agni
4. Rajasthan
5. Sitar
6. Emu
7. COARSE

MATHS AND IQ

1. 2401. The consecutive exponents of the digit seven.

2. | 30 | Divide | 15 | Plus | 4 | Minus | 1 | = | 5 |

3. POD. RAN are the three central letters in the word CRANE, and POD are the central letters in the word SPODE.

4. 25 (Add the digits: 1+9+6+3+2+4=25, 3+2+9+1+3+7=25)

5. | 60 | Plus | 24 | Minus | 14 | Divided | 10 | = | 7 |

VOCABULARY

1. DAME
2. SEOUL
3. STREAM
4. TRAM
5. DIAL

SPEED

1. Bamboo
2. A crown
3. Twelve
4. Pakistan
5. Issac Newton
6. Satyajit Ray
7. In the sea—because of the salt.
8. Zambezi
9. Karnam Malleswari
10. Needles

SET 2

TAKE YOUR PICK

1. Apart from Venus, which planet rotates from east to west?
   a. Jupiter
   b. Mars
   c. Uranus

2. Which country was Herodotus referring to when he said: 'There is no country that possesses so many wonders, nor any, that such a number of works that defy description'?
   a. China
   b. Germany
   c. Egypt

3. Which famous world leader was accused at the Rivonia Trial?
   a. Martin Luther King
   b. Subhas Chandra Bose
   c. Nelson Mandela

4. In Hindu mythology, who has a mansion named Vaijayanta and a sword named Paranjaya?
   a. Vishnu
   b. Shiva
   c. Indra

5. What is parasol a kind of?
   a. Umbrella
   b. Footwear
   c. Bracelet

6. What was the pen name of William Sydney Porter?
   a. Mark Twain
   b. Oscar Wilde
   c. O' Henry

7. Which spice consists of the seed of the Myristica fragrans, a tropical evergreen tree?
   a. Cardamom
   b. Clove
   c. Nutmeg

8. Which leader wrote the *Srimad Bhagavad Gita Rahasya* while he was jailed in Myanmar?
   a. Bal Gangadhar Tilak
   b. Motilal Nehru
   c. Gopal Krishna Gokhale

9. Who was born in Gwalior in 1945 to Haafiz Ali Khan?
   a. Amjad Ali Khan
   b. Bismillah Khan
   c. Ali Akbar Khan

10. Which is the largest internal organ in the human body?
    a. Liver
    b. Heart
    c. Lung

WHAT'S THE QUESTION

1. He is assisted by a group of fellow outlaws known as the 'Merry Men'.
2. Workers, drones and queens
3. Dadamoni
4. Anemometer
5. The first Swede male tennis player to become world number one in the Open era.
6. It is an arrangement of straps placed over an animal's snout.
7. It is a curved piece of wood that can be thrown so that it will return to the thrower.
8. It was built by Gustave Eiffel for the Universal Exposition of 1889, celebrating the centenary of the French Revolution.
9. Boxing Day
10. Jellystone National Park

MIXED BAG

1. Donna Berta di Bernardo left 60 'coins' in her will to Opera Campanilis Petrarum Sancte Marie to buy stones for which tower?
2. Which musician was the music director of the film *Mr & Mrs Iyer*?
3. In *Jack and the Beanstalk*, what was Milky White?
4. In Sikkim, the name of which mountain means 'Five Treasures of the Great Snow'?
5. *Raga Mala* is the autobiography of which famous Indian musician?

6. Why didn't Alexander Graham Bell's mother or his wife use the telephone he invented?
7. How many miles can a full-grown ostrich fly?
8. In terms of the currency notes of India, if MG Series is Mahatma Gandhi Series, what is AP Series?
9. What were originally sold as waist overalls?
10. What is the colour of the Golden Gate Bridge in San Francisco?

SPOT THE ANSWER

1. Who is a cruciverbalist?
    a. An expert at solving crossword puzzles
    b. A person who talks too much
    c. A tightrope walker

2. Kiran Bedi was once a champion in which sport?
    a. Kabaddi
    b. Tennis
    c. Karate

3. Why was the motto 'Be Prepared' chosen for the Boy Scout Movement?
    a. They were Baden-Powell's favourite two words.
    b. For no reason. Just for kicks.
    c. Based on the initials (BP) of its founder

4. How is Princess Manikarnika better known in history?
    a. Steffi Graf (her childhood nickname)
    b. Laika, the first dog in space
    c. Rani Lakshmibai of Jhansi

5. Who resides at 221B, Baker Street?
   a. Dennis the Menace
   b. Popeye
   c. Sherlock Holmes

CONFIDENCE ROUND

1. In 1992, who captained Pakistan to a Cricket World Cup victory?
2. How many days are there in 144 hours?
3. To attain perfect bliss is to attain: nirvana or yoga?
4. Normally, a violin has four, six or eight strings?
5. Which Indian delivered a speech in Chicago in 1893?
6. What means 'mixed bits' in Chinese: chowmein or chop suey?
7. The name of which country starts with 'E' and ends in 'T'?
8. Name the 'park' that John Hammond built on Isla Nublar.
9. The English title of which Salman Khan starrer was *When Love Calls*?
10. In the Ramayana, who was Dasaratha's eldest son?

WHAT'S THE WORD

Set 1

1. Common vampire, winged vampire and hairy-legged vampire are species of which mammal?
2. In literature, which little girl went to Wonderland?
3. What is the chemical symbol of potassium: P or K?
4. Which word announces the end of the first part in a

cinema: interval or interchange?
5. Mount Cook is in New Zealand or Australia?
6. Who was an Italian patriot: Guevara or Garibaldi?
7. What is the word?

Set 2

1. What does 'B' in VIBGYOR stand for: blue or brown?
2. Who saw forty thieves: Ali Baba or Aladdin?
3. Who was married to Raja Gangadhar Rao: Rani Padmini or Rani of Jhansi?
4. Who became chief minister earlier: Sheila Dikshit or Rabri Devi?
5. Which three letters are used as an abbreviation for 'et cetera'?
6. In December 2000, an informal contract was written on a napkin by Charly Rexach to sign which player for FC Barcelona?
7. What is the word?

Set 3

1. The term black panther is generally applied to leopards or lemurs?
2. The name of which part of the human body comes before brow, lash and lid?
3. In which country was Alfred Nobel born?
4. What kind of chips are mostly used in computers: silicon or iron?
5. If 'Z' is the last letter in the English alphabet, then, what is the last letter in the Greek alphabet?
6. Against which team did Sachin Tendulkar score his

only century at the 2003 Cricket World Cup?
7. What is the word?

Set 4

1. All trolleys have wheels: agree or disagree?
2. Who is also known as the Grand Old Man of India: Dadabhai Naoroji or Lala Lajpat Rai?
3. Which state has no coastline: Madhya Pradesh or West Bengal?
4. Who was a character in Shakespeare's *Othello*: Iago or Shylock?
5. What is the state animal of Sikkim?
6. In cricket, under which head are wides, no balls and byes classified?
7. What is the word?

Set 5

1. Copernicus is one of the most prominent craters on the moon: agree or disagree?
2. Who succeeded Jahangir as the Mughal emperor of India?
3. Which word describes a story or film containing events that precede those of an existing work: prequel or sequel?
4. The country Portugal is in which continent?
5. In a leap year, which festival is celebrated on the 360th day of the Gregorian calendar?
6. In a cricket match, what determines which team bats first?
7. What is the word?

MATHS AND IQ

1. Insert the missing number:
   24   8
   39   13
   ?   18

2. What should logically replace the question marks?
   1 C   5 ?
   A 3   E ?

3. Fill in the blanks with either addition, subtraction, multiplication or division to figure out the correct answer. Go sequentially from left to right without following BODMAS.

10		30		4		32	=	5

4. Find the odd one out.
   RUGAS
   LEEST
   PORPEC
   NOBREZ

5. Fill in the blanks with either addition, subtraction, multiplication or division to figure out the correct answer. Go sequentially from left to right without following BODMAS.

45		3		10		2	=	7

VOCABULARY

1. Rearrange the letters of the word 'CHAIN' to get the name of a country.
2. Rearrange the letters of the word 'MAUL' (as in

being mauled or eaten by a tiger) to get the name of a white-ish mineral used to purify water or to stop bleeding of cuts.
3. Rearrange the letters of the word 'TABLE' to get the sound a sheep makes.
4. Read the word 'BUS' backwards to get a prefix meaning lower.
5. Read the word 'NOW' backwards to get the basic monetary unit of North and South Korea.

SPEED

1. Which word relating to a geometric figure comes from two Latin words meaning 'around' and 'to carry'?
2. Which metal is alloyed with tin to form bronze?
3. The dance form Kuchipudi originated in West Bengal: serious or joking?
4. The Bhavani Talwar belonged to which famous Indian ruler?
5. A crore is ten million: serious or joking?
6. Which colour forms the background of the flag of the UN?
7. Who is the elder daughter of actress Tanuja?
8. Against which country does Australia play the Border–Gavaskar Test series?
9. What is the Sri Darbar Sahib better known as?
10. Which author's original name was Dhanpat Rai?

ANSWERS

TAKE YOUR PICK

1. Uranus
2. Egypt
3. Nelson Mandela
4. Indra
5. Umbrella
6. O' Henry
7. Nutmeg
8. Bal Gangadhar Tilak
9. Amjad Ali Khan
10. Liver

WHAT'S THE QUESTION

1. Who is Robin Hood?
2. Name three types of honeybees.
3. What was actor Ashok Kumar's nickname?
4. Which instrument is used to measure the speed of wind?
5. Who is Björn Borg?
6. What is a muzzle?
7. What is a boomerang?
8. Why was the Eiffel Tower erected?
9. What is the day after Christmas popularly known as?
10. In which park do Yogi Bear and Boo Boo live?

MIXED BAG

1. Leaning Tower of Pisa
2. Zakir Hussain
3. The name of the cow that Jack traded for some beans.
4. Kanchenjunga
5. Pandit Ravi Shankar
6. They were both deaf.
7. The ostrich cannot fly.
8. Ashokan Pillar Series
9. Jeans
10. Orange

SPOT THE ANSWER

1. An expert at solving crossword puzzles
2. Tennis. She won the Junior Lawn Tennis Championship in 1966, Asian Lawn Tennis Championship in 1972, and the All-India Hard Court Tennis Championship in 1974.
3. Based on the initials (BP) of its founder
4. Rani Lakshmibai of Jhansi
5. Sherlock Holmes

CONFIDENCE ROUND

1. Imran Khan
2. Six
3. Nirvana
4. Four
5. Swami Vivekananda

6. Chop suey
7. Egypt
8. Jurassic Park
9. *Maine Pyar Kiya*
10. Rama

WHAT'S THE WORD

Set 1

1. Bat
2. Alice
3. K
4. Interval
5. New Zealand
6. Garibaldi
7. BAKING

Set 2

1. Blue
2. Ali Baba
3. Rani of Jhansi
4. Rabri Devi
5. Etc.
6. Lionel Messi
7. BARREL

Set 3

1. Leopards
2. Eye
3. Sweden
4. Silicon

5. Omega
6. Namibia
7. LESSON

Set 4

1. Agree
2. Dadabhai Naoroji
3. Madhya Pradesh
4. Iago
5. Red Panda
6. Extras
7. ADMIRE

Set 5

1. Agree
2. Shah Jahan
3. Prequel
4. Europe
5. Christmas
6. Toss
7. ASPECT

MATHS AND IQ

1. 54 ($8 \times 3 = 24$, $13 \times 3 = 39$, so $18 \times 3 = 54$)
2. 1   C   5   G
   A   3   E   7

   Every alternate letter starting from A and its numeric position in the alphabet is given.

3. | 10 | Plus | 30 | Multiply | 4 | Divide | 32 | = | 5 |

4. RUGAS (SUGAR). All the others are metals or alloys— STEEL, COPPER, BRONZE.

5. | 45 | Divide | 3 | Minus | 10 | Plus | 2 | = | 7 |

VOCABULARY

1. CHINA
2. ALUM
3. BLEAT
4. SUB
5. WON

SPEED

1. Circumference
2. Copper
3. Joking. It originated from Andhra Pradesh.
4. Shivaji
5. Serious
6. Blue
7. Kajol
8. India
9. The Golden Temple
10. Munshi Premchand

SET 3

TAKE YOUR PICK

1. After whom is the chemical element with atomic number 102 named?
   a. Albert Einstein
   b. Alfred Bernhard Nobel
   c. Isaac Newton

2. In the Mahabharata, who was granted a divine inward eye so that he could see and relate the events of the battlefield to Dhritarashtra?
   a. Sanjaya
   b. Purochana
   c. Shikhandi

3. The capital of which Scandinavian country is located on the islands of Zealand and Amager?
   a. Norway
   b. Sweden
   c. Denmark

4. Complete this Sunderlal Bahuguna phrase which he coined during the Chipko Movement: 'Ecology is permanent ____.'
   a. Economy
   b. Sociology
   c. Biology

5. By what name is K'ung Fu-tzu better known to the Western world?
   a. Confucius
   b. Lao Tzu
   c. Fa-Hien

6. Which spice was introduced to India around 1800 CE by the East India Company in its spice garden in Courtallam, Tamil Nadu?
   a. Clove
   b. Pepper
   c. Cardamom

7. In *Twenty Thousand Leagues Under the Sea*, what was the name of the warship in which Captain Nemo sailed?
   a. Basillus
   b. Nautilus
   c. Remolus

8. Bidriware derives its name from the town of Bidar. In which state is Bidar located?
   a. Karnataka
   b. Kerala
   c. Gujarat

9. In India, who heads the Department of Space?
   a. The president
   b. The prime minister
   c. The defence minister

10. Which actor won the National Award in the Best Actor category for *Dastak* in 1971 and *Koshish* in 1973?
    a. Dev Anand
    b. Sanjeev Kumar
    c. Dilip Kumar

WHAT'S THE QUESTION

1. It is a piece of paper which indicates that you have paid for something.
2. Hypotenuse
3. A. S. Dileep Kumar (Hint: Music)
4. In the Ramayana, she was Lakshmana and Shatrughna's mother.
5. Aqua regia
6. Duodenum, jejunum and ileum
7. This husk, used to aid digestion, is commercially produced from *P. ovata* and *P. psyllium* in Pakistan and India.
8. This device is a blend of a modulator and a demodulator.
9. Talons
10. This tool is called a jack.

MIXED BAG

1. The motto 'If you desire peace, cultivate justice' is associated with which organisation?
2. In 2001, who became the first Indian girl to be the world junior chess champion?

3. In 1806, which typist's time saver was patented by Ralph Wedgwood?
4. In 1945, who shared the Nobel Prize in medicine with Howard Florey and Ernst Chain?
5. The Russians know this as Kaspiyskoye More. How is it known to us?
6. Which character by Charles Dickens is famous for his request: 'Please sir, may I have some more'?
7. What are brood parasites?
8. The twenty-five windows in which monument symbolise the gemstones found on Earth?
9. What food makes the cartoon character Popeye strong?
10. Which famous Kushan ruler was referred to as Chia-ni-se-chia in Chinese?

SPOT THE ANSWER

1. Why did the British settle in houseboats in Kashmir?
   a. They were barred from buying land to convert into resorts
   b. To protect their daughters from mixing with 'locals'
   c. The city was too congested and dirty

2. In 1906, which word was first coined by Maganlal Gandhi in the South African journal *Indian Opinion*?
   a. Ahimsa
   b. Satyagraha
   c. Harijan

3. In Japan, who was called 'Maikeru Jakuson'?
   a. The eldest son of the emperor
   b. Michael Jackson
   c. Eldest daughter of the emperor

4. How did the Hope diamond get its name?
   a. It is named after Henry Philip Hope who owned it in the 1830s
   b. It is named by the person who first mined it
   c. It is named after the Hope River in New Zealand

5. Carl Lewis does not have his 100 metre gold medal from the 1984 Olympics. Why?
   a. He lost it while swimming in the Niagara Falls.
   b. He donated it to UNICEF.
   c. He put it in his father's coffin.

CONFIDENCE ROUND

1. Kalidas wrote in Sanskrit or Tamil?
2. The presence of which element makes the blood red: iron or copper?
3. According to legend, which instrument did Nero play while Rome burnt?
4. Salt is used to preserve food: serious or joking?
5. The Solang Valley is in Himachal Pradesh or Arunachal Pradesh?
6. A cycling competition is usually held in: an aerodrome or a velodrome?
7. If you used your hand to play a 'harmonium', what would you use to play a 'harmonica'?

8. Which Nobel Prize winner was a teacher at St Mary's High School, Kolkata, from 1931 to 1948?
9. Which film director was awarded the Bharat Ratna in 1992?
10. Which mythical ruler had the 'golden touch'?

WHAT'S THE WORD

Set 1

1. Which is a shade of purple: tan or mauve?
2. Which king adopted the policy of 'conquest by dharma': Samudragupta or Ashoka?
3. The cricket team of which country has been named after its national flower, proteas?
4. In Greece, what is 'feta' a type of: cheese or butter?
5. The stripes of which animal are sometimes called 'follow me' stripes helping the young ones follow their mothers through the forest: giraffe or okapi?
6. Which set of cards, used in fortune telling, is divided into two groups called Major Arcana and Minor Arcana?
7. What is the word?

Set 2

1. With which sport is a 'dohyo' associated: sumo or judo?
2. Which of these is a snake-like fish: an eel or a seal?
3. Which ornament is worn around the neck: a bracelet or a choker?
4. In the official name of India, what comes before India: Republic or Union?

5. The River Volga flows through which continent?
6. Which Hindi film actress' sister is Farah Naaz?
7. What is the word?

Set 3

1. Which Indian prime minister was the son of another Indian prime minister?
2. In the country UAE, what does 'E' stand for: Empire or Emirates?
3. In Pakistan, what is a rupee divided into: paisa or cent?
4. How many arms does an octopus have?
5. *The Night Watch* was one of which painter's most well-known paintings?
6. What is the costume of a female ballet dancer called: Tutu or Tunic?
7. What is the word?

Set 4

1. Which game gets its name from the public school in Warwickshire, England, where it was first played: Rugby or Cricket?
2. Harry Potter could talk to snakes: agree or disagree?
3. In the abbreviation NATO, what does 'N' stand for?
4. Which capital city of India is also known as the 'adobe of Drona'?
5. The name of which fruit comes from the Arabic word *naranj*?
6. Which Dessau-born scholar was the son of the Romantic poet Wilhelm Müller?
7. What is the word?

Set 5

1. Which religious leader died at Kushinagar: Buddha or Mahavira?
2. What is the hard covering of the crown of teeth called: enamel or canine?
3. The characters Sheriff Woody, Buzz Lightyear and Mr Potato Head appear in which animated film series?
4. What is the name of the cylindrical clay oven in which naans are made: tandoor or kadhai?
5. In which country is the Aswan High Dam located?
6. Which of these was the first man-made fibre: Rayon or Rubber?
7. What is the word?

MATHS AND IQ

1. An anagram of this author's name is, very aptly, 'I'll make a wise phrase'. Who is he?
2. An express train leaves Kolkata for Mumbai at the same time as a passenger train leaves Mumbai for Kolkata. Which is farther from Kolkata when they meet? (Express train average speed: 60 km/hr; Passenger train average speed: 30 km/hr)
3. Fill in the blanks with either addition, subtraction, multiplication or division to figure out the correct answer. Go sequentially from left to right without following BODMAS.

| 15 | | 4 | | 7 | | 62 | = | 5 |

4. 100 cats killed 100 rats in three minutes. How many minutes did three cats take to kill three rats?

5. Fill in the blanks with either addition, subtraction, multiplication or division to figure out the correct answer. Go sequentially from left to right without following BODMAS.

85		36		7		1	=	7

VOCABULARY

1. Rearrange the letters of the word 'DAWN' to get what magicians sometimes use.
2. Rearrange the letters of the word 'CLAM' to get a word meaning serene.
3. Rearrange the letters of the word 'SHORE' to get an animal.
4. Read the word 'KEEP' backwards to get a four-letter word meaning to take a brief look at something.
5. Read the word 'DEED' backwards to get a word that means 'an act or action'.

SPEED

1. Which great Indian leader's surname sounds like a religious mark on the forehead?
2. Who played the role of Itzhak Stern in the 1993 film *Schindler's List*?
3. Spider, hermit and horseshoe are varieties of which creature?
4. The India Gate is in Mumbai: serious or joking?
5. In India, which sport is played in Durand Cup?
6. What is informally called a chopper: a tram or a helicopter?

7. Who was the first prime minister of India to receive the Bharat Ratna?
8. What carries blood away from the heart?
9. What is measured on a spring balance?
10. From which famous town did the Pied Piper take away all the children?

ANSWERS

TAKE YOUR PICK

1. Alfred Bernhard Nobel
2. Sanjaya
3. Denmark
4. Economy
5. Confucius
6. Clove
7. Nautilus
8. Karnataka
9. The prime minister
10. Sanjeev Kumar

WHAT'S THE QUESTION

1. What is a receipt?
2. In a right-angled triangle, what do you call the side opposite the right angle?
3. What is music composer A. R. Rahman's real name?
4. In the Ramayana, who was Sumitra?
5. What is the popular name for a mixture of concentrated nitric and hydrochloric acids, used for dissolving gold?
6. Name the three parts of the small intestine.
7. What is isabgol?
8. What is a modem?
9. What are a bird of prey's hooked claws called?

10. What tool is used to raise a car when a tyre needs changing?

MIXED BAG

1. ILO (International Labour Organization)
2. Koneru Humpy
3. Carbon paper
4. Alexander Fleming
5. Caspian Sea
6. Oliver Twist
7. Birds that lay their eggs in other birds' nests and have the foster parents take care of them, e.g. cuckoo.
8. The Statue of Liberty
9. Spinach
10. Kanishka

SPOT THE ANSWER

1. They were barred from buying land to convert into resorts
2. Satyagraha
3. Michael Jackson (Maikeru is Japanese for Michael)
4. It is named after Henry Philip Hope who owned it in the 1830s
5. He put it in his father's coffin

CONFIDENCE ROUND

1. Sanskrit
2. Iron

3. The fiddle
4. Serious
5. Himachal Pradesh
6. Velodrome
7. Hands and lips
8. Mother Teresa
9. Satyajit Ray
10. Midas

WHAT'S THE WORD

Set 1
1. Mauve
2. Ashoka
3. South Africans
4. Cheese
5. Okapi
6. Tarot cards
7. MASCOT

Set 2
1. Sumo
2. Eel
3. Choker
4. Republic
5. Europe
6. Tabu
7. SECRET

Set 3
1. Rajiv Gandhi

2. Emirates
3. Paisa
4. Eight
5. Rembrandt
6. Tutu
7. REPORT

Set 4
1. Rugby
2. Agree
3. North
4. Dehradun
5. Orange
6. Max Müller
7. RANDOM

Set 5
1. Buddha
2. Enamel
3. The *Toy Story* series
4. Tandoor
5. Egypt
6. Rayon
7. BETTER

MATHS AND IQ
1. William Shakespeare
2. Neither. When they meet they will be the same distance from Kolkata.
3.

| 15 | Multiply | 4 | Plus | 7 | Minus | 62 | = | 5 |

4. Three minutes
5. | 85 | Minus | 36 | Divide | 7 | Multiply | 1 | = | 7 |

VOCABULARY

1. WAND
2. CALM
3. HORSE
4. PEEK
5. DEED

SPEED

1. Bal Gangadhar Tilak
2. Ben Kingsley
3. Crabs
4. Joking; it is in New Delhi
5. Football
6. Helicopter
7. Jawaharlal Nehru
8. The arteries
9. Weight
10. Hamelin

SET 4

TAKE YOUR PICK

1. Adams, Leverrier, Galle and Lassell are some of the rings of which planet?
   a. Neptune
   b. Saturn
   c. Jupiter
2. In the Mahabharata, who among these was killed by Krishna?
   a. Karna
   b. Ekalavya
   c. Jayadratha
3. Which famous philosopher was also the tutor of Alexander the Great?
   a. Aristotle
   b. Socrates
   c. Rousseau
4. What was defined as 'three grains of barley, dry and round, placed end to end lengthwise'?
   a. Centimetre
   b. Millimetre
   c. Inch
5. The name of which of these means the 'gilded one' in Spanish?
   a. El Dorado

b. Buenos Aires
   c. El Nino
6. Which 1852 book was smuggled into Russia in Yiddish to evade the czarist censor?
   a. *Uncle Tom's Cabin*
   b. *Alice in Wonderland*
   c. *Das Kapital*
7. Who was the prime minister of the United Kingdom at the time of Queen Elizabeth II's coronation?
   a. Neville Chamberlain
   b. Winston Churchill
   c. Harold McMillan
8. Tomato, sweet corn, oxtail, bird's nest, chimney and French onion are all …
   a. Types of soup
   b. Breeds of cats
   c. Sporting events
9. Which work is often referred to as the fifth veda?
   a. *Panchtantra*
   b. *Natyashastra*
   c. *Arthshastra*

10. Which Indi-pop singer was born Sujata, and was known for her hit 'Made in India'?
    a. Sunita Rao
    b. Alisha Chinai
    c. Pravati Khan

WHAT'S THE QUESTION

1. In *Winnie the Pooh*, she is Roo's mother.

2. He directed the film *Kuch Kuch Hota Hai*.
3. Harmattan
4. Varicella
5. The author of *A House for Mr Biswas*
6. In Western astrology, it is the second sign of the zodiac.
7. Mezzanine
8. Howard Carter
9. This country was once known as South West Africa.
10. Hydrophobia is its other name.

MIXED BAG

1. Why were copper rivets put on denim jeans?
2. The name of which country, situated partly in Europe and partly in Asia, is also the name of a bird?
3. Which scientist was offered the presidency of Israel after Chaim Weizmann's death in 1952?
4. During the construction of which monument was a small town called Mumtazabad built for the workers?
5. Which famous novel begins with the words 'Call me Ishmael'?
6. My father won a Padma Bhushan in 1976, my wife won a Padma Shri in 1992 and I have received a Padma Shri, a Padma Bhushan and a Padma Vibhushan. Who am I?
7. In *Tintin* comics, who is called Milou in French?
8. Which popular song during the War of American Independence is the republic's unofficial national anthem?
9. The north Indian drink *kanji* is normally made with

a vegetable whose scientific name is *Daucus carota sativis*. How is this vegetable better known?
10. Which cricketer played the role of a villain in the film *Kabhi Ajnabi The*?

SPOT THE ANSWER

1. For what was a Kashmiri natural dye called 'rattanjog' previously used?
   a. To dye the shawl pashmina
   b. To give the dish roganjosh its red colour
   c. It was mixed with mehendi for dyeing hair

2. What does an ichthyologist study?
   a. The cause of itch and other skin diseases
   b. Fish
   c. Comics

3. What is a croissant?
   a. A crescent-shaped (bread-like) roll made of yeast
   b. A cross-stitch in embroidery
   c. An African spider

4. Who is a shoeblack?
   a. He removes the make-up of actresses.
   b. The correct term for a person who polishes shoes for a living.
   c. He looks after the slippers/shoes of coal miners.

5. Which present-day city was established by Dost Mohammed Khan in 1724?

a. Bhopal
b. Kanpur
c. Udaipur

CONFIDENCE ROUND

1. Who was the first Indian to win the Miss Universe title?
2. Who is the first Indian prime minister to hold office for more than one term?
3. If you aren't careful, in which of these games can you go bankrupt: Ludo or Monopoly?
4. Which is longer: the small or the large intestine?
5. S.D. Burman composed the music for *Sholay*: serious or joking?
6. Which capital city was formerly called Pataligram and Kusumpur?
7. Which is the longest of the five tributaries of the Indus river?
8. Who was the author of *Hitopadesha*?
9. In India, how many digits comprise the PNR number on a railway ticket?
10. Which world famous magician shares his name with the title character of a Charles Dickens novel?

WHAT'S THE WORD

Set 1

1. Where does tartar accumulate: teeth or toes?
2. Who was older: Ashok Kumar or Kishore Kumar?
3. What is a religious teacher of the Jewish community

called: a rabbi or a synagogue?
4. Who became the secretary of the Ahmedabad Textile Labour Association in 1992: Gulzarilal Nanda or Indira Gandhi?
5. What number batsman comes to bat after the sixth wicket falls?
6. Which state is famous for Tanjore paintings?
7. What is the word?

Set 2

1. Which country has a tricolour flag with white, blue and red bands: Canada or Russia?
2. What name is commonly given to the code of polite behaviour in society: epithet or etiquette?
3. Which surname is shared by the man who discovered Tutankhamun's tomb and the thirty-ninth US president: Carter or Clinton?
4. Biju Patnaik and his son Naveen Patnaik have been chief ministers of which Indian state?
5. In human blood, cells of which colour carry haemoglobin?
6. Commonly, which seven-letter name is given to a microcomputer suitable for use at an ordinary desk?
7. What is the word?

Set 3

1. Which of these is usually not encased in a shell: a walnut or a raisin?
2. What are most reptiles classified as: ectothermic or endothermic?
3. Dr John Watson is the companion of which fictional

character?
4. In India, what does 'I' in CBI stand for: investigation or intelligence?
5. Which five-letter word meaning 'magnificent' comes before Canyon and Slam?
6. Who was the famous mother of Sanjay Dutt?
7. What is the word?

Set 4

1. A parakeet is a seed eating parrot or woodpecker?
2. Which actress acted in Gurinder Chadha's *Bride and Prejudice*: Sushmita Sen or Aishwarya Rai?
3. Which fairy-tale character is famous for her long hair: Cinderella or Rapunzel?
4. In which Indian state is the annual Pushkar Fair held: Haryana or Rajasthan?
5. Which month gets its name from the Latin word for 'eight'?
6. Which cuddly toy was invented in honour of Theodore Roosevelt?
7. What is the word?

Set 5

1. What are bristol and bond two grades of: cheese or paper?
2. Grapes can also be black in colour: agree or disagree?
3. Which capital do Punjab and Haryana share: Srinagar or Chandigarh?
4. Which temperature scale is named after the British physicist William Thomson?
5. Which word is used to describe two objects or places at equal distances?

6. In computers, what is a program designed to breach security in the guise of performing some harmless function called?
7. What is the word?

MATHS AND IQ

1. Which is the odd one out and why?
   NEALPT, BRIBTA, XLAGYA, MCEOT
2. Fill in the blanks with either addition, subtraction, multiplication or division to figure out the correct answer. Go sequentially from left to right without following BODMAS.

   | 25 | | 5 | | 55 | | 7 | = | 10 |

3. Insert the word that completes the first word and starts the next. (Clue: Animal) C (...) X
4. If DRIVER = 7 PEDESTRIAN = 11 Then, ACCIDENT =?
5. Fill in the blanks with either addition, subtraction, multiplication or division to figure out the correct answer. Go sequentially from left to right without following BODMAS.

   | 36 | | 2 | | 24 | | 8 | = | 12 |

VOCABULARY

1. Rearrange the letters of the word 'NOSE' to get the name of a river in Bihar.
2. Rearrange the letters of the word 'RAP' to get a golfing term.
3. Rearrange the letters of the word 'WHAT' to get a

word to describe the melting of snow.
4. Read the word 'REWARD' backwards to find a compartment in your desk.
5. Read the word 'RATS' backwards to find a heavenly body.

SPEED

1. In the nursery rhyme *Hey Diddle Diddle*, who ran away with the spoon?
2. A meteorologist studies meteors: serious or joking?
3. Which country did Moses lead his people out of?
4. Which is not a martial art: kung fu, ikebana or judo?
5. Which continent has half the world's population?
6. Snoopy and Charlie Brown appear in which comic strip, which has an edible name?
7. Only female *Anopheles* mosquitoes can transmit malaria or dengue?
8. What was the most common colour of tennis balls before yellow was introduced?
9. Louis Braille was born blind: serious or joking?
10. From where did Shivaji escape by hiding inside a basket: Lucknow or Agra?

ANSWERS

TAKE YOUR PICK

1. Neptune
2. Ekalavya
3. Aristotle
4. Inch
5. El Dorado
6. *Uncle Tom's Cabin*
7. Winston Churchill
8. Types of soup
9. *Natyashastra*
10. Alisha Chinai

WHAT'S THE QUESTION

1. Who is Kanga?
2. Who is Karan Johar?
3. What is the name of a well-known West African trade wind?
4. What is the medical term for chicken pox?
5. Who is V.S. Naipaul?
6. What is Taurus?
7. What do you call the storey of a building which is between the two main floors?
8. Name the British archaeologist who discovered the largely intact tomb of King Tutankhamen.
9. By what name was Namibia formerly known?

10. By what other name is rabies known?

MIXED BAG

1. To prevent the pockets from tearing under the weight of tools and to increase their durability.
2. Turkey
3. Albert Einstein
4. Taj Mahal
5. *Moby Dick*
6. Amitabh Bachchan
7. Snowy
8. Yankee Doodle
9. Carrot
10. Syed Kirmani (It also featured cricketer Sandip Patil.)

SPOT THE ANSWER

1. To give the dish *roganjosh* its red colour
2. Fish
3. A crescent-shaped (bread-like) roll made of yeast
4. The correct term for a person who polishes shoes for a living
5. Bhopal

CONFIDENCE ROUND

1. Sushmita Sen
2. Jawaharlal Nehru
3. Monopoly
4. Small intestine

5. Joking. The music was composed by his son R.D. Burman.
6. Patna
7. Sutlej
8. Narayana Pandit
9. Ten
10. David Copperfield

WHAT'S THE WORD

Set 1

1. Teeth
2. Ashok Kumar
3. Rabbi
4. Gulzari Lal Nanda
5. Eight
6. Tamil Nadu
7. TARGET

Set 2

1. Russia
2. Etiquette
3. Carter; Howard Carter and Jimmy Carter
4. Odisha
5. Red
6. Desktop
7. RECORD

Set 3

1. Raisin
2. Ectothermic

3. Sherlock Holmes
4. Investigation
5. Grand
6. Nargis
7. RESIGN

Set 4

1. Parrot
2. Aishwarya Rai
3. Rapunzel
4. Rajasthan
5. October
6. Teddy bear
7. PARROT

Set 5

1. Paper
2. Agree
3. Chandigarh
4. Kelvin scale
5. Equidistant
6. Trojan Horse
7. PACKET

MATHS AND IQ

1. BRIBTA (RABBIT—an animal). The others are associated with space—COMET, GALAXY, PLANET.

2. | 25 | Multiply | 5 | Minus | 55 | Divided | 7 | = | 10 |

3. APE

4. 9 (DRIVER has 6 letters +1 = 7, PEDESTRIAN has 10 letters + 1=11, ACCIDENT has 8 letters+1=9)

5. | 36 | Multiply | 2 | Plus | 24 | Divided | 8 | = | 12 |

VOCABULARY

1. SONE
2. PAR
3. THAW
4. DRAWER
5. STAR

SPEED

1. The dish
2. Joking; he studies the atmosphere and weather
3. Egypt
4. Ikebana
5. Asia
6. *Peanuts*
7. Malaria
8. White
9. Joking; he lost his vision by the age of three
10. Agra

SET 5

TAKE YOUR PICK

1. Which of these elements is not named after a scientist?
   a. Einsteinium
   b. Ruthenium
   c. Curium

2. In which present-day country was the Battle of Waterloo fought?
   a. France
   b. Iran
   c. Belgium

3. Which rakshasa took the form of a golden deer to lure Lakshmana away, leaving Sita unprotected?
   a. Tadaka
   b. Mareecha
   c. Nikumbha

4. In India, 'Duty Unto Death' is the motto of which organization?
   a. Border Security Force
   b. National Cadet Corps
   c. Central Bureau of Investigation

5. Which country's highest peak is Mount Ararat?
   a. China
   b. Turkey
   c. Iran

6. What do you call a system of serving when a meal, consisting of several dishes is set out and guests serve themselves?
   a. Buffet
   b. A la carte
   c. Menu

7. With which artist would you associate *The Thinker,* a statue cast in bronze?
   a. Auguste Rodin
   b. Michelangelo
   c. Leonardo da Vinci

8. Kisan Ghat in Delhi is the memorial ground of which famous leader?
   a. Charan Singh
   b. Rajiv Gandhi
   c. Jagjivan Ram

9. Edward Lear was famous for his five-line humorous poems. What is the correct term for this style of poetry?
   a. Elegy
   b. Sonnet
   c. Limerick

10. Which character did actor Leonard Nimoy portray in *Star Trek V: The Final Frontier*?
    a. Spock
    b. Kirk
    c. McCoy

WHAT'S THE QUESTION

1. This is where leather is produced from animal skins.
2. It was the last capital of the kingdom of Vijayanagar.
3. Collage
4. In a 1982 film, he came to Earth and wanted to call home.
5. The SI unit of energy or work is named after this scientist.
6. Anastasia and Drizella (Hint: Children's literature)
7. This J-shaped elastic sac is the widest part of the digestive system.
8. In comics, Lothar is his best friend and crime-fighting companion.
9. Hellas
10. Chandigarh was planned by this French architect.

MIXED BAG

1. Which river is the largest drainage system in the world in terms of the volume of its flow and the area of its basin?
2. Issued by Sweden, what kind of an object is the Treskilling Yellow?
3. Whose most well-known poems are contained in the

collection *Barrack-Room Ballads*?
4. In 1961, which Indian state was liberated from Portuguese rule?
5. In which state of India is the only floating national park in the world located?
6. Ivan Lendl and Martina Navratilova represented USA in international competitions later in their careers. Which country did they originally belong to by birth?
7. Whose sacred tooth is said to be at Sri Lanka's Temple of the Tooth?
8. Supremo, a famous comic-strip character of the 1980s, was styled after which Hindi film actor?
9. With which Indian community would you associate the dal-meat preparation called 'dhansak'?
10. The word 'hygiene' is named after the Greek goddess of what?

SPOT THE ANSWER

1. If you were staying at 'The Y', where would you be staying?
   a. The YMCA
   b. The headquarters of Mahesh Yogi
   c. Yamini Krishnamurthy's Dance Academy

2. How did Mount Everest get its name?
   a. After Sir George Everest, the then Surveyor General of India
   b. After the Greek god of mountains
   c. Edmund Hillary's childhood nickname was 'Everest'

3. Who among these is most likely to use a gavel?
   a. Pilot
   b. Judge
   c. Puppeteer

4. What did Pingali Venkaiah design, which was adopted by India's Constituent Assembly on 22 July 1947?
   a. The Indian National Flag
   b. Madhuri Dixit's costumes in Khalnayak
   c. The Rashtrapati Bhavan

5. On what grounds was Surendranath Banerjee's admission to the Indian Civil Service (now IAS) rejected?
   a. He misrepresented his age
   b. His IQ was below fifty-five
   c. Because only women were allowed in the ICS

CONFIDENCE ROUND

1. Which four-letter word is used to describe the male protagonist of a film?
2. Who was the first woman to win the Nobel Prize?
3. Which animal has been on the logo of WWF since 1961?
4. Which country is known for its dykes: Holland or Spain?
5. Which character was created by Charles Dickens: Oliver Twist or Tom Brown?
6. The local name of the Indian wild dog sounds like which percussion instrument?
7. Which London-based football club has been coached

by Arsene Wenger?
8. Which cookery show host wrote *Khazana of Indian Vegetarian Recipes*?
9. Pakistan has a larger population than Russia: serious or joking?
10. Who had a horse named Bucephalus?

WHAT'S THE WORD

Set 1

1. Which steel city lies along the Damodar river: Bokaro or Bilaspur?
2. Which of these is the largest living bird: ostrich or rhea?
3. Most skyscrapers are vertical or horizontal?
4. Which superhero was born in Long Island, New York, to Howard Anthony Stark and Maria Collins Carbonell Stark?
5. During which festival are snakes worshipped: Nag Panchami or Raksha Bandhan?
6. How many unit lengths will you use moving from minus 1 to 7?
7. What is the word?

Set 2

1. Which of these are more in number: countries or continents?
2. Which of these is the capital of Peru: Santiago or Lima?
3. What is a dome-shaped Eskimo house, typically built from blocks of solid snow, called?
4. Kim Jong-il was a leader of which country: South

Korea or North Korea?
5. Give me a four-letter word for 'a soft, white substance formed when milk sours, used as the basis for cheese'.
6. Which of these parts of the human body serves as a pump: kidney or heart?
7. What is the word?

Set 3

1. What are bowler and sombrero types of?
2. Which river is called *Nahr al Furat* in Arabic: Jordan or Euphrates?
3. In which city is the Lord's cricket ground located: Manchester or London?
4. Which rock constitutes an estimated 95 per cent of the upper part of the Earth's crust: igneous or sedimentary?
5. Which scheduled language of India is an official language of Pakistan?
6. According to the proverb, what does a rolling stone not gather?
7. What is the word?

Set 4

1. Ra is the chemical symbol of which element?
2. Which of these organisations has France and Belgium as its members: European Union or OPEC (Organization of Petroleum Exporting Countries)?
3. Ants can lift and carry more than three times their own weight: serious or joking?
4. Which Indian prime minister was born on 4 December

1919, in Jhelum?
5. In Hindu mythology, who was Lakshmana's father?
6. Conjunctiva is a part of which organ of the human body?
7. What is the word?

Set 5

1. In which language was the Ramayana originally composed: Hindi or Sanskrit?
2. Which district is in the state of Uttar Pradesh: Etah or Bellary?
3. Which nut is shaped like a bean: chestnut or cashew nut?
4. What is also known as lockjaw: tetanus or conjunctivitis?
5. The scientific name of which bird is *Struthio camelus*?
6. Which flower is the symbol of the British Labour Party?
7. What is the word?

MATHS AND IQ

1. Find the number that logically completes the series: 2, 3, 5, 9, 17, _____
2. Use the digit '4' four times and the bracket, addition, subtraction, multiplication or division symbols to make the digit 3.
3. Fill in the blanks with either addition, subtraction, multiplication or division to figure out the correct answer. Go sequentially from left to right without following BODMAS.

| 54 | | 34 | | 10 | | 5 | = | 10 |

4. A zookeeper was asked to count the number of birds and animals in a zoo. He counted thirty heads and a hundred feet. Find the number of birds and the number of animals in the zoo.
5. Fill in the blanks with either addition, subtraction, multiplication or division to figure out the correct answer. Go sequentially from left to right without following BODMAS.

| 33 | | 11 | | 43 | | 34 | = | 12 |

VOCABULARY

1. Rearrange the letters of the word 'SPICE' to describe books like the Ramayana and Mahabharata.
2. Rearrange the letters of the word 'PETAL' to find something on the dining table.
3. Rearrange the letters of the word 'RESIST' to get a member of your family.
4. Read the word 'GUM' backwards to get a drinking vessel.
5. Read the word 'TIDE' backwards to get a word that means to prepare for publication by correcting or modifying written material.

SPEED

1. What do you call the result of multiplying two numbers?
2. Who was born earlier: Albert Einstein or Isaac Newton?

3. When you add a post-script to a letter, which two letters of the alphabet do you use?
4. Mount Godwin Austen is also known as M2 or K2?
5. Which colour is used to describe cinema tickets bought illegally?
6. In which country was Sir Donald Bradman born?
7. Which famous Dickens character's stepfather was Mr Edward Murdstone?
8. Flying foxes are bats: serious or joking?
9. Where would you find your palm: hand or leg?
10. Bahadur Shah II was the last ruler of which dynasty?

ANSWERS

TAKE YOUR PICK

1. Ruthenium. Ruthenium is named after a region of central Europe, Curium is named after the Curies, Einsteinium is named after Einstein.
2. Belgium
3. Mareecha
4. Border Security Force
5. Turkey (Greater Ararat)
6. Buffet
7. Auguste Rodin
8. Charan Singh
9. Limerick
10. Spock

WHAT'S THE QUESTION

1. What is a tannery?
2. What is Hampi?
3. What do you call a piece of art made by sticking different materials such as photographs and pieces of paper or fabric on to a surface?
4. Who was the lovable alien ET?
5. Who was James Prescott Joule?
6. Who were Cinderella's stepsisters?
7. What is the stomach?
8. Who is Mandrake?

9. What is the Greek name for Greece and appears on its stamps?
10. Who was Le Corbusier?

MIXED BAG

1. Amazon
2. Stamp
3. Rudyard Kipling
4. Goa
5. Manipur. Keibul Lamjao National Park
6. Czechoslovakia
7. Gautama Buddha
8. Amitabh Bachchan
9. Parsis
10. Health

SPOT THE ANSWER

1. The YMCA. The Young Men's Christian Association is a world-wide Christian voluntary movement for women and men, seeking to build a community based on love, peace and reconciliation.
2. After Sir George Everest, the then Surveyor General of India. Sir George Everest was the Surveyor General of India in 1830–1843. He is credited with completing the trigonometric survey of India. Mount Everest was renamed in his honour, from Peak XV, in 1865.
3. Judge
4. The Indian National Flag
5. He misrepresented his age

CONFIDENCE ROUND

1. Hero
2. Marie Curie
3. Giant panda
4. Holland; dykes are embankments built to prevent flooding from the sea.
5. Oliver Twist
6. Dhol. The name of the dog is Dhole.
7. Arsenal
8. Sanjeev Kapoor
9. Serious; Pakistan's population is 196,174,380 (est) while Russia's is 142,470,272 (est).
10. Alexander

WHAT'S THE WORD

Set 1

1. Bokaro
2. Ostrich
3. Vertical
4. Iron Man
5. Nag Panchami
6. Eight
7. BOVINE

Set 2

1. Countries
2. Lima
3. Igloo
4. North Korea

5. Curd
6. Heart
7. CLINCH

Set 3

1. Hats
2. Euphrates
3. London
4. Igneous
5. Urdu
6. Moss
7. HELIUM

Set 4

1. Radium
2. European Union
3. Serious
4. I.K. Gujral
5. Dasharatha
6. Eye
7. RESIDE

Set 5

1. Sanskrit
2. Etah
3. Cashew nut
4. Tetanus
5. Ostrich
6. Rose
7. SECTOR

MATHS AND IQ

1. 33 (2+1=3, 3+2=5, 5+4=9, 9+8=17, 17+16=33)
2. 3= (4+4+4)/4
3. | 54 | Minus | 34 | Divided | 10 | Multiply | 5 | = | 10 |
4. Birds=10, Animals=20
5. | 33 | Divide | 11 | Plus | 43 | Minus | 34 | = | 12 |

VOCABULARY

1. EPICS
2. PLATE
3. SISTER
4. MUG
5. EDIT

SPEED

1. The product
2. Isaac Newton
3. P.S.
4. K2
5. Black
6. Australia
7. David Copperfield
8. Serious
9. Hand
10. Mughal

SET 6

TAKE YOUR PICK

1. Collectively, how many moons do the planets Mercury and Venus have?
   a. One
   b. None
   c. Fifty-five

2. The Chinese pilgrim Fa-hien visited Kannauj between 399 and 414 A. D. during the reign of...
   a. Chandragupta II
   b. Ashoka
   c. Kanishka

3. Which deity is credited with teaching Ayurveda to Sushruta?
   a. Vishwakarma
   b. Dhanwantari
   c. Charaka

4. In which device might you come across a trackball?
   a. TV camera
   b. Computer
   c. Watch

5. What island did Peter Minuit acquire for sixty guilders from the Native Americans?

a. Manhattan Island
   b. Christmas Island
   c. Galapagos Island

6. Which of these herbs, used extensively in Indian cuisine, is referred to as *dhania* in Hindi?
   a. Coriander
   b. Fenugreek
   c. Asafoetida

7. Sir Winston Churchill visited which country during its years under British rule and called it 'the pearl of Africa'?
   a. Somalia
   b. Uganda
   c. South Africa

8. Jatra is a traditional theatre form of which state of India?
   a. Andhra Pradesh
   b. West Bengal
   c. Maharashtra

9. Abraham Ortelius's book, *Theatrum Orbis Terrarum*, which means 'Theatre of the World', is generally believed to be the first modern example of what?
   a. Atlas
   b. Dictionary
   c. Encyclopedia

10. Which of these Raj Kapoor starrers was also released

as *The Vagabond*?
a. *Barsaat*
b. *Awara*
c. *Shri 420*

WHAT'S THE QUESTION

1. In Roman numerals it is expressed as MXC.
2. This Mughal emperor was born in Fergana in 1483.
3. Pedicure
4. In the Mahabharata, she was the only sister of Duryodhana.
5. Victor, Laverne and Hugo
6. The lady in this painting is thought to be Lisa Gherardini.
7. Khyber Pass
8. In 1962, John Glenn Jr was the first man to do this.
9. Shatabdi Express was flagged off in 1988 to commemorate his 100th birth anniversary.
10. Alopecia is the medical term.

MIXED BAG

1. Lord Krishna was born when Vishnu sent a black hair into Devaki's womb. Who was born when he sent a white hair into Rohini's womb?
2. The region of Macau, which was a colony of Portugal till 1999 is now part of which country?
3. In India, which leader's death anniversary is celebrated as Anti-Terrorism Day?
4. In the *Secret Seven* books, what is the name of Peter

and Janet's golden spaniel?
5. In 1661, which Indian city was given to King Charles II as part of the dowry when he married Princess Catherine de Braganza of Portugal?
6. Which fruit is also known as Chinese gooseberry?
7. Nadia Comaneci was the first woman to obtain a perfect 10 in Olympic gymnastics. Who was the first man?
8. What did Gutzon Borglum and his son Lincoln leave behind in the Black Hills of South Dakota, USA?
9. I was popularly known as M.S. I was born in Madurai. I received the Bharat Ratna in 1998. Who am I?
10. Which film by Satyajit Ray was completed when Dr B.C. Roy, former chief minister of West Bengal, provided funds from the Public Works Department, on the grounds that 'path' was a matter within the PWD's jurisdiction?

SPOT THE ANSWER

1. Why was champion swimmer Dawn Fraser banned from competitions for many years?
    a. She stole a flag from the Emperor's Palace at the Tokyo Olympics.
    b. She tested positive for drugs.
    c. She was a 'man' participating as a woman.

2. What is a leveret?
    a. A machine to lift heavy weight
    b. The young of a hare
    c. A remote control

3. Euphemistically, what is a 'marble orchard'?
   a. A shop which sells coloured playing marbles
   b. A graveyard, because of the marble tombstones
   c. A toilet decorated with glazed tiles

4. In India, if the Green Revolution referred to grains, and the White Revolution to milk, what did the Blue Revolution refer to?
   a. Tourism
   b. Production of fish
   c. Production of Indigo

5. What was the Bombay Pentangular?
   a. The five-storied Kapoor home
   b. A pre-Independence cricket tournament
   c. The five top film studios before Independence

CONFIDENCE ROUND

1. What do the number of dots on all six faces of a dice add up to?
2. Which religious place is famous for its Assi and Rewan Ghats: Sarnath or Varanasi?
3. In which country was Florence Nightingale born?
4. What is a four-letter word for a killer whale?
5. What is the STD code for New Delhi?
6. Which comet is named after a contemporary of Sir Isaac Newton?
7. Against which team did Steve Waugh make his Test debut: England or India?
8. When Jacob and Wilhelm first published them, they

were called *Children's and Household Tales*. How are these stories better known today?
9. Who was the leading lady in M.F. Hussain's *Meenaxi: A Tale of Three Cities*?
10. The sound of an elephant can be associated with which musical instrument?

WHAT'S THE WORD

Set 1

1. The characters Gru and Dr Nefario appear in which animated film series?
2. The FIFA Congress in Barcelona in 1929 assigned which country as the first host country of the FIFA World Cup: Bolivia or Uruguay?
3. Which variety of kebab was apparently invented by a highly skilled chef for a toothless Nawab of Lucknow: Shami kebab or Galouti kebab?
4. Where do the Wallace's flying frogs live almost exclusively: trees or oceans?
5. The name of which continent starts with the fifth letter of the alphabet?
6. In Indian railways, what does the letter 'R' in 'RAC' stand for?
7. What is the word?

Set 2

1. What does 'D' in the title 'D. Litt' stand for: doctor or director?
2. Which of these has a milk base: yoghurt or shikanji?
3. Hoshangabad and Jabalpur are situated on the banks

of which river?
4. The name of which animal is a Spanish word meaning 'little armored one'?
5. In the human body, striated, cardiac and smooth are all types of_____
6. Which epic by Homer deals with the wanderings of Odysseus after the fall of Troy?
7. What is the word?

Set 3

1. Which of these comes before the official name of Australia: Commonwealth or Republic?
2. Which of these cities is in Rajasthan: Udaipur or Ooty?
3. What lens would your grandfather use to correct his short sightedness: concave or convex?
4. Which niece of Rishi Kapoor made her debut opposite Abhishek Bachchan: Kareena Kapoor or Karishma Kapoor?
5. Which small word describes 'a pole with a blade used for rowing or steering a boat'?
6. Which is a citrus fruit: orange or banana?
7. What is the word?

Set 4

1. Ricky Ponting's nickname is Punter: agree or disagree?
2. Normally, in a pack of fifty-two playing cards, how many kings would you find?
3. What are Old Glory and Jolly Roger names of: flags or birds?

4. Quito is the capital of which country?
5. What is a rag doll made of?
6. What is an abnormally rabid heart rate called: tachycardia or thoracotomy?
7. What is the word?

Set 5

1. Which word describes 'a member of a sports team in their first full season': rookie or cookie?
2. Asmara is the capital of which country: Eritrea or Libya?
3. Which is the Maori word for 'peaks on the back': tarantula or tuatara?
4. Who look the same: fraternal twins or identical twins?
5. Which word derived from the Latin word for 'new' describes 'a star showing a sudden large increase of brightness'?
6. In many countries, what is the first day of the fourth month of the Gregorian calendar called?
7. What is the word?

MATHS AND IQ

1. Simplify this: The day before day after the day after the day before yesterday.
2. Fill in the blanks with either addition, subtraction, multiplication or division to figure out the correct answer. Go sequentially from left to right without following BODMAS.

| 6 | | 9 | | 7 | | 95 | = | 10 |

3. Does the last statement follow the first two?

a. Marion is an Italian.
   b. Marion sings beautifully.
   c. All Italians sing beautifully.
4. Mr and Mrs Smith had seven sons. Each had a sister. How many people were there in the Smith family?
5. Fill in the blanks with either addition, subtraction, multiplication or division to figure out the correct answer. Go sequentially from left to right without following BODMAS.

| 50 | | 15 | | 5 | | 1 | = | 12 |

VOCABULARY

1. Rearrange the letters of the word 'THROW' to get a word meaning value.
2. Rearrange the letters of the word 'ALSO' to find an Asian country.
3. Rearrange the letters of the word 'NEST' to get a kind of gun.
4. Read the word 'DESSERTS' (as in puddings) backwards, what word do you get?
5. Read the word 'YAM' backwards to get the name of a month.

SPEED

1. If tea is made from leaves, what is coffee made from?
2. What is the study of flags called?
3. Wales is a part of United Kingdom: serious or joking?
4. How many years are there in three decades?
5. In the acronym ESP, what does 'E' stand for?

6. Who created Sherlock Holmes: P.D. James or Arthur Conan Doyle?
7. The mridangam is a wind, percussion or stringed instrument?
8. What does 'merci' mean when translated from French to English?
9. How many seconds are there in a day?
10. Who was evil: Dr Jekyll or Mr Hyde?

ANSWERS

TAKE YOUR PICK
1. None
2. Chandragupta II
3. Dhanwantari
4. Computer. It is a small ball that is set in a holder, and can be rotated by hand to move a cursor on a computer screen.
5. Manhattan Island
6. Coriander
7. Uganda
8. West Bengal
9. Atlas
10. *Awara*

WHAT'S THE QUESTION

1. How would you express the number 1090 in Roman numerals?
2. Who was Babur?
3. What is the term used to describe the process of caring for and beautifying the feet?
4. Who was Dushala?
5. Who were Quasimodo's three gargoyle friends in the Walt Disney film *The Hunchback of Notre Dame*?
6. What is the *Mona Lisa*?
7. Name the most northerly pass that connects Pakistan and Afghanistan.

8. Who was the first US astronaut to orbit the Earth?
9. Who was Jawaharlal Nehru?
10. What is the medical term for baldness?

MIXED BAG

1. Balabhadr (Balarama, Baladeva)
2. China
3. Rajiv Gandhi
4. Scamper
5. Mumbai
6. Kiwi
7. Alexander Dityatin
8. The carved heads of former US presidents George Washington, Thomas Jefferson, Abraham Lincoln and Theodore Roosevelt at Mount Rushmore
9. M.S. Subbulakshmi
10. *Pather Panchali*

SPOT THE ANSWER

1. She stole a flag from the Emperor's palace at the Tokyo Olympics
2. The young of a hare
3. A graveyard, because of the marble tombstones
4. Production of fish
5. A pre-Independence cricket tournament

CONFIDENCE ROUND
1. Twenty-one
2. Varanasi

3. Italy
4. Orca
5. 011
6. Haley's Comet, after Edmund Haley
7. India
8. Grimms' Fairy Tales
9. Tabu
10. The trumpet

WHAT'S THE WORD

Set 1

1. *Despicable Me*
2. Uruguay
3. Shami kebab
4. Trees
5. Europe
6. Reservation
7. DUSTER

Set 2

1. Doctor
2. Yoghurt
3. Narmada
4. Armadillo
5. Muscles
6. *Odyssey*
7. DYNAMO

Set 3

1. Commonwealth

2. Udaipur
3. Concave
4. Kareena Kapoor
5. Oar
6. Orange
7. CUCKOO

Set 4
1. Agree
2. Four
3. Flags
4. Ecuador
5. Cloth
6. Tachycardia
7. AFFECT

Set 5
1. Rookie
2. Eritrea
3. Tuatara
4. Identical twins
5. Nova
6. April Fools' Day
7. RETINA

MATHS AND IQ

1. Yesterday
2. | 6 | Plus | 9 | Multiply | 7 | Minus | 95 | = | 10 |
3. No
4. Ten (Each brother had the same sister.)

5. | 50 | Plus | 15 | Divided | 5 | Minus | 1 | = | 12 |

VOCABULARY

1. WORTH
2. LAOS
3. STEN
4. STRESSED
5. MAY

SPEED

1. Beans
2. Vexillology
3. Serious
4. Thirty
5. Extra (Extra Sensory Perception)
6. Arthur Conan Doyle
7. Percussion
8. Thank you
9. 86400
10. Mr Hyde

SET 7

TAKE YOUR PICK

1. Which is the only giant planet whose equator is nearly at right angles to its orbit?
   a. Mars
   b. Jupiter
   c. Uranus

2. The archeological remains of which institution is found in the vicinity of a village called 'Bara Gaon' in the eastern part of India?
   a. Nalanda University
   b. Taxila University
   c. Ujjain Sun Temple

3. In the Mahabharata, which grandson of Pandu died in warfare when he was trapped in a 'Chakravyuha'?
   a. Abhimanyu
   b. Prativindhya
   c. Yaudheya

4. In Buddhism, what among these does the 'swastika' signify?
   a. Buddha's feet or footprints
   b. Teachings of Buddha
   c. Signature of Buddha

5. Which style of cooking shares its name with the second largest province of China?
   a. Hunan
   b. Szechwan
   c. Shandong

6. Sri Jayawardenepura Kotte is the legislative and judicial capital of which country?
   a. Maldives
   b. Sri Lanka
   c. Seychelles

7. Shakti Sthal is the samadhi of which prime minister of India?
   a. Jawaharlal Nehru
   b. Charan Singh
   c. Indira Gandhi

8. 'Yakshagana' is a traditional theatre form of which Indian state?
   a. Maharashtra
   b. Andhra Pradesh
   c. Karnataka

9. Which famous author's original name was Charles Lutwidge Dodgson?
   a Enid Blyton
   b. Lewis Carroll
   c. Charles Dickens

10. In which film has Michelle McNally's story been

memorably told?
a. *Black*
b. *Family*
c. *Hum Tum*

WHAT'S THE QUESTION

1. Isthmus
2. Ornithology
3. Moat
4. Château
5. In India, it is popularly known as imli.
6. Tinker Bell's friend who never grew up
7. Gossima and then ping-pong
8. A comic-strip character whose car is registered with the number 313.
9. Louis and Auguste Lumière
10. The Potala Palace is the winter residence of this religious leader.

MIXED BAG

1. The capital of which Indian state is named after Ananthan, the cosmic serpent with a thousand heads?
2. Which famous dancer founded Kalakshetra at Adyar in Chennai?
3. Work out the four-letter name of this animal. The first two letters make a verb. The first three an Indian state. The last three a cereal plant and the last two a preposition.
4. Which famous monument is the tomb of Muhammad

Adil Shah?
5. Who was the commander of the Pandava forces during the battle of Kurukshetra?
6. In 1865, the first edition of which book by an English mathematician was withdrawn because of bad printing?
7. Spiridon Louis won the marathon gold in the first modern Olympics at Athens in 1896. Which country did he represent?
8. The name of which country was coined by Choudhry Rahmat Ali and is said to be an acronym formed from Punjab, Afghania, Kashmir, Sind and Baluchistan?
9. I played a blind school principal in the 1980 film *Sparsh* and a professor in the 1993 film *Sir*. Who am I?
10. Which cuisine, introduced during the reign of Nawab Asaf-ud-Daulah, literally means 'choking off the steam'?

SPOT THE ANSWER

1. Arabica and Robusta are two main varieties of what?
   a. Horse
   b. Coffee
   c. Biryani

2. What became an Olympic event in 1912 at the Stockholm Games?
   a. Women's Swimming
   b. Canoe sprinting
   c. Basketball

3. What is fly ash?
   a. Mosquitoes killed by repellents
   b. Aishwarya Rai's private helicopter
   c. Small dark flecks produced by the burning of powdered coal or other materials

4. Who founded the 'Heal the World Foundation', for the safety, health and development of children?
   a. Hillary Clinton
   b. Laloo Prasad Yadav
   c. Michael Jackson

5. Which famous Indian's ashes were lying in the main branch of the State Bank of India in Cuttack since 1950?
   a. Dr S. Radhakrishnan
   b. K.L. Saigal
   c. Mahatma Gandhi

CONFIDENCE ROUND

1. Which of these is a steamed dumpling filled with meat or vegetables: momo or pasta?
2. In India, which is the highest peacetime gallantry award: Param Vir Chakra or Ashok Chakra?
3. Normally, what happens to its temperature when an animal goes into hibernation?
4. Who was a Pakistani fast bowler: Danish Kaneria or Mohammad Sami?
5. Are horses herbivorous or carnivorous?
6. The famous Gahirmatha beach in Odisha is located

on which Indian coast: east or west?
7. Which Paul wrote the bestselling book *The Population Bomb*: Ehrlich or Wood?
8. What kind of tube sticks out from the front of a kettle: snout, spout or tout?
9. Encephalitis is a disease that affects the brain. Which part of your body is affected when you have hepatitis?
10. Who is an expert at conducting an orchestra: Zakir Hussain or Zubin Mehta?

WHAT'S THE WORD

Set 1

1. Florence Nightingale was born in Florence: agree or disagree?
2. The name of which animal comes from the Hindi words for 'blue' and 'cow'?
3. Which is the largest city in Australia?
4. Who wrote the famous poem *Daffodils*?
5. Which part of the human body has photoreceptors?
6. Which Indian president was the president of the Indian National Congress in 1934, 1939 and 1947?
7. What is the word?

Set 2

1. The Cardamom Hills are a part of the Western Ghats: agree or disagree?
2. In Hindi, which spice is known as *saunf*: fennel or fenugreek?
3. On which day do tableau presentations normally take place in front of VIPs in New Delhi: Republic Day or

Independence Day?
4. Fe is the symbol of which chemical element?
5. In navigation or surveying, which is the primary device to find a direction on Earth?
6. Which eleven-letter word starting with 'A' is a magician's favourite word?
7. What is the word?

Set 3

1. In India, what did the Blue Mutiny refer to: indigo or rice?
2. Ne is the chemical symbol of which element?
3. All planets in the solar system are named after gods of Greek mythology: serious or joking?
4. Where is the archaeological site Sarnath located: Madhya Pradesh or Uttar Pradesh?
5. Which train first ran between Delhi and Howrah in 1969: Duronto or Rajdhani?
6. Which worm is also called angleworm?
7. What is the word?

Set 4

1. Spaniels are so called because they apparently originated in Spain: serious or joking?
2. In the abbreviation www, what does the third 'w' stand for: wide or web?
3. Which Southeast Asian country was formerly known as Dutch East Indies?
4. Which spice is the dried, cleaned and polished rhizome of *Curcuma longa*: tamarind or turmeric?
5. Which famous leader was Rajmohan Gandhi's

maternal grandfather?
6. The Greek word for sun, *helios*, was used in naming which element?
7. What is the word?

Set 5

1. As a prefix, 'sub' means under or over?
2. Which blood cells carry oxygen to body tissues: red blood cells or white blood cells?
3. Which continent has both the highest and the lowest points on the surface of the Earth?
4. Who became the president of South Africa in 1994?
5. In mythology, Shakuni was Duryodhana's uncle or grandfather?
6. What word connects the following clues: dwarfs, wonders and continents?
7. What is the word?

MATHS AND IQ

1. How much mud is there in a hole 1 foot by 2.5 feet by 3.75 feet?
2. Gloria has twelve right-hand gloves and fifteen left-hand gloves in a drawer. How many gloves should she take out to be sure of taking out at least one of each hand?
3. Fill in the blanks with either addition, subtraction, multiplication or division to figure out the correct answer. Go sequentially from left to right without following BODMAS.

| 5 | | 2 | | 50 | | 4 | = | 15 |

4. Find the next number in the sequence: 8, 15, 29, 57, _____

5. Fill in the blanks with either addition, subtraction, multiplication or division to figure out the correct answer. Go sequentially from left to right without following BODMAS.

| 45 | | 5 | | 10 | | 13 | = | 6 |

VOCABULARY

1. Rearrange the letters of the word 'POST' to put an end to motion.
2. Rearrange the letters of the word 'CARPEL' to get a word for goods wrapped up in a package.
3. Rearrange the letters of the word 'DUST' to find a place where horses are bred.
4. Read the word 'STRAW' backwards to get a hard, rough growth on the surface of the skin.
5. Read the word 'EMIT' backwards to get a unit of measurement.

SPEED

1. In *The Thousand and One Nights*, who recounts his adventures on seven voyages: Sindbad or Aladdin?
2. Which country is referred to as Druk-Yul meaning 'Land of the Thunder Dragon' in their local language?
3. Is the scapula above or below the femur?
4. How long will it take a car to travel 150 km at an

average speed of 30 kmph?
5. Who was the captain of the 1983 team which won the Cricket World Cup for India?
6. How many legs does a camera tripod have?
7. Bats hang upside down when asleep: serious or joking?
8. How many metres make a kilometre: 100 or 1,000?
9. Which brothers achieved the first powered, sustained, and controlled airplane flight?
10. In Indian history, who was the famous wife of Raja Gangadhar Rao?

ANSWERS

TAKE YOUR PICK

1. Uranus
2. Nalanda University
3. Abhimanyu
4. Buddha's feet or footprints
5. Szechwan
6. Sri Lanka
7. Indira Gandhi
8. Karnataka
9. Lewis Carroll
10. *Black*

WHAT'S THE QUESTION

1. What do you call a narrow strip of land with sea on either side, joining two larger masses of land?
2. What do you call the scientific study of birds?
3. What do you call a trench filled with water that surrounds a castle?
4. What is a large French country house or castle called?
5. What is the Indian (Hindi) name for tamarind?
6. Who is Peter Pan?
7. What was the original name of table tennis?
8. Who is Donald Duck?
9. Who were the creators of the first motion picture?

10. Who is Dalai Lama?

MIXED BAG

1. Kerala
2. Rukmini Devi Arundale
3. Goat
4. Gol Gumbaz
5. Dhrishtadyumna. He was Draupadi's brother.
6. *Alice's Adventures in Wonderland*
7. Greece
8. Pakistan
9. Naseeruddin Shah
10. Dum pukht

SPOT THE ANSWER

1. Coffee
2. Women's Swimming
3. Small dark flecks produced by the burning of powdered coal or other materials
4. Michael Jackson
5. Mahatma Gandhi. They were finally immersed in the holy Sangam in Allahabad.

CONFIDENCE ROUND

1. Momo
2. Ashok Chakra
3. It decreases
4. Mohammad Sami

5. Herbivorous
6. East
7. Ehrlich
8. Spout
9. The liver
10. Zubin Mehta

WHAT'S THE WORD

Set 1
1. Agree
2. Nilgai
3. Sydney
4. William Wordsworth
5. Eyes
6. Rajendra Prasad
7. ANSWER

Set 2
1. Agree
2. Fennel
3. Republic Day
4. Iron
5. Compass
6. Abracadabra
7. AFRICA

Set 3
1. Indigo
2. Neon
3. Joking

4. Uttar Pradesh
5. Rajdhani Express
6. Earthworm
7. INJURE

Set 4

1. Serious
2. Web
3. Indonesia
4. Turmeric
5. C. Rajagopalachari
6. Helium
7. SWITCH

Set 5

1. Under
2. Red blood cells
3. Asia
4. Nelson Mandela
5. Uncle
6. Seven
7. URANUS

MATHS AND IQ

1. There is no mud in a hole.
2. Sixteen
3.

| 5 | Multiply | 2 | Plus | 50 | Divide | 4 | = | 15 |

4. 99 (Beginning with 7, even multiples of 7 are added to the previous number to get the next number.)

5. | 45 | Divide | 5 | Plus | 10 | Minus | 13 | = | 6 |

VOCABULARY

1. STOP
2. PARCEL
3. STUD
4. WARTS
5. TIME

SPEED

1. Sindbad
2. Bhutan
3. Above
4. Five hours
5. Kapil Dev
6. Three
7. Serious
8. 1,000
9. The Wright brothers
10. Rani Lakshmibai/Rani of Jhansi

SET 8

TAKE YOUR PICK

1. Fill in the blank: the wheel and axle, the lever, the ramp, the screw and the pulley are all_____ machines.
   a. Simple
   b. Turbine
   c. Mechanical components

2. According to Hindu mythology, which snake killed Parikshit?
   a. Kaliya
   b. Takshak
   c. Ananta

3. In which city can you find the mausoleum of Arjumand Bano Begum?
   a. Delhi
   b. Agra
   c. Aurangabad

4. What is described in the Oxford English Dictionary as 'an Indian sweet made from a mixture of flour, sugar, and shortening, which is shaped into a ball'?
   a. Rasgulla
   b. Laddu
   c. Balushahi

5. The name of which city comes from two words meaning 'market for areca nut' in the local language?
   a. Guwahati
   b. Kohima
   c. Itanagar

6. In geometry, which figure gets its name from the Greek word for 'table'?
   a. Rhombus
   b. Square
   c. Trapezeum

7. Who wrote the science fiction classic *Rendezvous with Rama*?
   a. Arthur C. Clarke
   b. Ray Bradbury
   c. H.G. Wells

8. The life of which deity makes up the most common theme of Pahadi paintings?
   a. Buddha
   b. Narada
   c. Krishna

9. Who was the first woman to be appointed the governor of Uttar Pradesh?
   a. Sucheta Kripalani
   b. Sarojini Naidu
   c. Vijaya Lakshmi Pandit

10. 15 August 2005 marked the thirtieth anniversary of

which path-breaking film?
a. *Deewar*
b. *Mughal-e-Azam*
c. *Sholay*

WHAT'S THE QUESTION

1. This fictional character has been played by Sean Connery, David Niven, George Lazenby and Roger Moore on screen.
2. According to the Western zodiac, the name of this constellation means 'goat-horned' in Latin.
3. 'Mitrabhed' and 'Mitralabh' are two of the five chapters of this famous work by Vishnu Sharma.
4. 8,611 metres, making it the second highest mountain in the world.
5. This element was so named because Cyprus was the chief source.
6. Filigree
7. Mintonette
8. A naked winged boy with a bow and arrows
9. The Swedish Academy, The Norwegian Committee, The Royal Swedish Academy of Sciences and The Assembly at Karolinska Institutet
10. Gowalia Tank Maidan, Mumbai (now called August Kranti Maidan)

MIXED BAG

1. In 1590, the Portuguese first sighted the island of Taiwan. What did they name it?

2. For which famous monument is Ustad Isa credited?
3. Which is the only member of the cat family to live in groups called prides?
4. What is common to cheddar, mozzarella, edam and camembert?
5. The Rigveda Samhita is divided into ten books. What are the books called?
6. What is the main ingredient in a finger bowl?
7. In which capital city would you find the famous Temple of the Emerald Buddha?
8. In World War II, what was code-named 'Operation Barbarossa'?
9. We were born as Arthur Stanley Jefferson and Oliver Norvell Hardy. We are a famous comedy pair. How are we better known?
10. Who was the first woman to fly solo across the Atlantic Ocean?

SPOT THE ANSWER

1. The Incas had no form of writing, instead, they had relay runners conveying messages by carrying what they called 'quipus'. What were quipus?
   a. Double-sided mirrors
   b. Knotted designs of human hair
   c. Colour-coded arrangements of knotted threads

2. Which king called himself 'Devanampiya Piyadasi' or 'beloved of the gods and handsome in looks'?
   a. Ashoka
   b. Prithviraj Chauhan

c. Maharana Pratap

3. Of what are A4 and B5 sizes?
    a. Diamond
    b. CD-Roms
    c. Paper

4. In 1804, the Cathedral of Notre Dame in Paris witnessed the crowning ceremony of...
    a. Alexander the Great
    b. Napoleon Bonaparte
    c. Louis XVI

5. Why is House 54 on University Avenue, in Rangoon, a big tourist attraction?
    a. It was the house where Aung San Suu Kyi was kept under house arrest
    b. It is the site of the world's largest pagoda
    c. Lord Mountbatten's grave is located there

CONFIDENCE ROUND

1. Marble cakes are actually made of marble: serious or joking?
2. Which Leo wrote the books *Anna Karenina* and *War and Peace*?
3. If the flamenco is a dance form, what is a flamingo?
4. In Hindu mythology, who was Pandu's wife: Kunti or Gandhari?
5. Which tiny particle has about the same mass as a proton: neutron or electron?

6. Which Indian state is bordered by Pakistan and the states of Rajasthan, Madhya Pradesh and Maharashtra?
7. Which actress made her debut in the film *Pardes*: Shilpa Shetty or Mahima Choudhary?
8. Are ants classified as social, anti-social or socialist insects?
9. The Vidarbha Cricket Association Stadium is located in which city in Maharashtra: Ahmedabad or Nagpur?
10. Which part of the word 'bifocals' means two?

WHAT'S THE WORD

Set 1

1. Which of these European nations is an island: Georgia or Malta?
2. Clementines, tangerines and cara caras are types of which fruit?
3. Which scientist is more famous for his works on gravity: Newton or Herschel?
4. Which director would you associate with the films *Hero No. 1* and *Coolie No. 1*: David Dhawan or Mahesh Bhatt?
5. Who is the author of the book *Wings of Fire*?
6. Which part of the egg is also called deutoplasm?
7. What is the word?

Set 2

1. Which grow faster: fingernails or toenails?
2. Which boy's name is spoken in radio communication to convey that the message has been understood:

Roger or Rover?
3. In which continent does the River Po flow: Africa or Europe?
4. Which chemical element was first identified as a unique element in 1751 by Baron Axel Fredrik Cronstedt: Nickel or Copper?
5. Which spice is called *elaichi* in Hindi: cardamom or mustard?
6. Which Mughal ruler was also called Nasir-al-Din Muhammad?
7. What is the word?

Set 3

1. In *Gulliver's Travels*, what was Gulliver's first name: Lemuel or Samuel?
2. Hyder Ali was Tipu Sultan's father: agree or disagree?
3. Which of these is a marsupial: wombat or armadillo?
4. In *Tintin* comics, who was the Abominable Snowman?
5. Which cricket stadium is named after Lord Auckland's sisters: Eden Gardens or Green Park?
6. In which state of india is the Hawa Mahal located?
7. What is the word?

Set 4

1. In which of these films have Hema Malini and Amitabh Bachchan appeared together: *Baghban* or *Kal Ho Naa Ho*?
2. The auditory ossicles are located in which organ of the human body?
3. Which commentator has not played Test cricket: Ravi Shastri or Harsha Bhogle?

4. Which state is larger in terms of area: Arunachal Pradesh or Manipur?
5. In Tibet, which breed of dog is called 'abso seng kye'?
6. How many angles does a pentagon have?
7. What is the word?

Set 5

1. Which fruit is commonly used as flavouring in golgappas: tamarind or mango?
2. Which Indian bowler made his Test debut in Australia: L. Balaji or Irfan Pathan?
3. What is the first name of the Indian painter M.F. Hussain: Mian or Maqbool?
4. The Ganges flows through Bihar or Tamil Nadu?
5. Which is the third planet from the sun and the fifth largest in our solar system?
6. Under Peter the Great, which country was proclaimed an empire in 1721: Italy or Russia?
7. What is the word?

MATHS AND IQ

1. Rearrange the letters and find the odd one: EMEPLT QUOMSE EHOSU HURHCC
2. Ravi's watch is ten minutes slow, though he thinks it is five minutes fast. Rohan's watch is five minutes fast though he thinks it is ten minutes slow. They both plan to catch a train at 4 p.m. Who gets their first: Ravi or Rohan?
3. Fill in the blanks with either addition, subtraction, multiplication or division to figure out the correct

answer. Go sequentially from left to right without following BODMAS.

| 13 | | 17 | | 28 | | 3 | = | 6 |

4. Assuming the truth of these sentences
   (a) Yellow dogs are live animals.
   (b) All live animals need food.
   Which of the following sentences is true?
   1) A dog is yellow because it needs food.
   2) All yellow dogs need food.
   3) Certain yellow dogs do not need food.
   4) Some yellow dogs are not live animals.
5. Fill in the blanks with either addition, subtraction, multiplication or division to figure out the correct answer. Go sequentially from left to right without following BODMAS.

| 3 | | 97 | | 10 | | 6 | = | 15 |

VOCABULARY

1. Rearrange the letters of the word 'GOAT' to get a Roman costume.
2. Rearrange the letters of the word 'CARE' to get a unit of land measurement.
3. Rearrange the letters of the word 'GAIN' to get a Hindu god.
4. Read the word 'FLOW' backwards to get an animal's name.
5. Read the word 'ABLE' backwards to get where Napoleon was exiled.

SPEED

1. Which actor was affectionately called 'Kaka': Rajesh Khanna or Shammi Kapoor?
2. Who was the 'chief' of the losing team at the Battle of Plassey?
3. It is called turmeric in English. What is it called in Hindi?
4. If you consume 0.264 gallons of milk, how many litres would you have consumed?
5. Which four-letter word represents the pointed top of a mountain?
6. Which teeth of yours sounds like a dog?
7. How many sides does a hexagon have?
8. Which country is the second largest producer of silk?
9. What is the state tree of Kerala?
10. Which satellite orbited the Earth first: Sputnik or Explorer I?

ANSWERS

TAKE YOUR PICK

1. Simple
2. Takshak
3. Agra
4. Laddu
5. Guwahati
6. Trapezeum
7. Arthur C. Clarke
8. Krishna
9. Sarojini Naidu
10. *Sholay*. It was released on 15 August 1975.

WHAT'S THE QUESTION

1. Who is James Bond?
2. What is Capricorn?
3. What is *Panchatantra*?
4. What is the height of the mountain K2 or Godwin Austen?
5. What is copper?
6. What term is used to describe the application of gold or silver on a surface in a fine pattern?
7. What was the original name of volleyball?
8. In Roman mythology, how is Cupid (the god of love) depicted?

9. Which organisations are responsible for awarding the Nobel Prizes every year?
10. Where did Gandhiji give his 'Quit India' call during the freedom movement?

MIXED BAG

1. Formosa
2. The Taj Mahal
3. Lion
4. All of these are varieties of cheese.
5. Mandalas
6. Water
7. Bangkok
8. The German attack on the (former) USSR in 1941
9. Laurel and Hardy
10. Amelia Earhart

SPOT THE ANSWER

1. Colour-coded arrangements of knotted threads. The colours of the cords, the way the cords are connected together, the relative placement of the cords, the spaces between the cords, the types of knots on the individual cords, and the relative placement of the knots are all part of theological-numerical recording.
2. Ashoka
3. Paper. In the ISO paper size system, all pages have a height-to-width ratio of the square root of two (1:1.4142).
4. Napoleon Bonaparte

5. It was the house where Aung San Suu Kyi was kept under house arrest. She won the Nobel Peace prize in 1991.

CONFIDENCE ROUND

1. Joking. It is a cake with a streaked or mottled appearance achieved by very lightly blending light and dark batter.
2. Leo Tolstoy
3. A bird
4. Kunti
5. Neutron
6. Gujarat
7. Mahima Choudhary
8. Social
9. Nagpur
10. Bi

WHAT'S THE WORD

Set 1
1. Malta
2. Orange
3. Newton
4. David Dhawan
5. A.P.J. Abdul Kalam
6. Yolk
7. MONDAY

Set 2

1. Fingernails
2. Roger
3. Europe
4. Nickel
5. Cardamom
6. Humayun
7. FRENCH

Set 3

1. Lemuel
2. Agree
3. Wombat
4. Yeti
5. Eden Gardens
6. Rajasthan
7. LAWYER

Set 4

1. *Baghban*
2. Ear
3. Harsha Bhogle
4. Arunachal Pradesh
5. Lhasa Apso
6. Five
7. BEHALF

Set 5

1. Tamarind
2. Irfan Pathan
3. Maqbool

4. Bihar
5. Earth
6. Russia
7. TIMBER

MATHS AND IQ

1. EHOSU (HOUSE). The others are public places of worship—TEMPLE, CHURCH, MOSQUE.
2. Rohan. He came earlier as his watch was fast.
3. | 13 | Plus | 17 | Minus | 28 | Multiply | 3 | = | 6 |
4. All yellow dogs need food.
5. | 3 | Plus | 97 | Minus | 10 | Divide | 6 | = | 15 |

VOCABULARY

1. TOGA
2. ACRE
3. AGNI
4. WOLF
5. ELBA

SPEED

1. Rajesh Khanna
2. Siraj-ud-daulah
3. *Haldi*
4. One litre
5. Peak
6. Canine
7. Six

8. India
9. Coconut palm
10. Sputnik

SET 9

TAKE YOUR PICK

1. Which fabric was introduced by Sir H.B. Lumsden and W. Hodson in 1848 for the uniforms of British colonial troops in India?
   a. Khaki
   b. Denim
   c. Corduroy

2. In Hindu mytholgy, who cursed Krishna that he would be killed by trickery?
   a. Kunti
   b. Gandhari
   c. Karna

3. M.K. Gandhi lived in a farm in South Africa named after a famous Russian novelist. Name the author.
   a. Leo Tolstoy
   b. Mark Twain
   c. Charles Dickens

4. Haflong is the only hill station of…
   a. Manipur
   b. Assam
   c. Meghalaya

5. Thomson seedless, bangalore blue, anab-e-shahi are the major varieties of which fruit in India?
   a. Grapes
   b. Oranges
   c. Litchis

6. In which book would you come across the floating island of Laputa and the land of the Houyhnhnms?
   a. *Robinson Crusoe*
   b. *Kidnapped*
   c. *Gulliver's Travels*

7. Which Indian dance form traces its traditions to the Mahari and the Gotipua traditions?
   a. Kathak
   b. Kathakali
   c. Odissi

8. Who among these advises the Government of India on legal matters?
   a. Attorney General
   b. Speaker of the Lok Sabha
   c. Governor of Reserve Bank of India

9. In 1976, in which catgeory did *Sholay* win its only Filmfare Award?
   a. Best Film
   b. Best Director
   c. Best Editing

10. Which are the only big cats to have a tuft or a bunch

of hair at the end of their tail?
a. Lions
b. Tigers
c. Jaguars

WHAT'S THE QUESTION

1. It is the currency of UAE.
2. La Marseillaise
3. The Golden Hind
4. Merci beaucoup
5. This theory explains that the universe began with a big explosion.
6. Green Goblin
7. Creutzfeldt-Jakob disease
8. A book called *Our Films, Their Films*
9. A painting called *Guernica*
10. A ball that reaches the batsmen without bouncing

MIXED BAG

1. Which is the southernmost capital city in the world?
2. In the Ramayana, which rakshasa was known as Jaya and served as Vishnu's gatekeeper at Vaikuntha?
3. A tigon is an offspring of a tiger and a lioness. What do you call the offspring of a lion and a tigress?
4. In which novel does Jean Valjean steal a loaf of bread and is imprisoned?
5. Upon completion in 1931, it was called the All India War Memorial. How do we know it today?
6. In 1974, who became the first Indian woman singer to

receive the Ramon Magsaysay award?
7. What was Abraham Lincoln referring to when he said, 'If I ever get a chance to hit that thing, I'll hit it hard'?
8. Which planet was predicted by a Frenchman named Le Verrier and an Englishman named John Adams?
9. Which Hollywood 1956 classic has the line, 'So let it be written, so it shall be done'?
10. In Kerala, if you are eating karimeen, what would you be eating?

SPOT THE ANSWER

1. The Chinese expression Kung Hei Fat Choi, means...
   a. Have a prosperous and happy new year
   b. Good luck for the quiz
   c. Happy birthday

2. In whose honour was 29 August chosen as National Sports Day in India?
   a. Milkha Singh's birthday
   b. Dhyan Chand's birthday
   c. Sunil Gavaskar's birthday

3. Some cough mixtures have the word 'linctus' in them, what is the origin of the term?
   a. Contains lime
   b. To be licked
   c. Contains linoleum

4. What is common to owls, aardvark, kiwi and bats?
   a. They all sleep on their backs.

b. They generally hunt at night.
   c. They were all used as Olympic mascots.

5. What would a Chinese individual do with a wok?
   a. Burst it (Chinese cracker)
   b. Eat it (Dumpling)
   c. Cook in it (Chinese cooking vessel)

CONFIDENCE ROUND

1. Which of these places did an American reach first: the moon or space?
2. How many faces does a cuboid have?
3. Which Indian poet is also known as Bharatendu?
4. Bronze is an alloy traditionally composed of copper and _____.
5. Cabbages are always green in colour: serious or joking?
6. Who is younger: Sourav Ganguly or Mohammad Kaif?
7. Which of these is a reptile: iguana or echidna?
8. Which mountain range is broadly divided into the Canadian, Northern, Middle and Southern?
9. What does the 'O' in OPEC stand for?
10. Where did Vasco da Gama establish the first Portuguese factory: Cochin or Visakhapatnam?

WHAT'S THE WORD

Set 1

1. Which flower has a trumpet-shaped centre: dahlia or daffodil?

2. Which team has won more hockey gold medals in the Olympics: India or Pakistan?
3. Which epic means the 'great epic of the Bharata dynasty' in Sanskrit: Ramayana or Mahabharata?
4. Which city shares its name with a Trojan prince: Rome or Paris?
5. Who among these is a fictional character in the novel *Treasure Island*: Long John Silver or Fagin?
6. Which name has been applied to Arctic people by Europeans: eskimo or yeti?
7. What's the word?

Set 2

1. What is a marmoset: monkey or parrot?
2. Sneezing is a reflex action of the human body: agree or disagree?
3. Which actress made a guest appearance in *Kal Ho Naa Ho*: Rani Mukherjee or Madhuri Dixit?
4. Majuli, one of the largest riverine islands in the world, is on which river?
5. In Hindu mythology, who was Sumitra's son: Lakshmana or Bharata?
6. Which landmark is in Paris: Eiffel Tower or Colosseum?
7. What is the word?

Set 3

1. Which country is landlocked: Mali or South Africa?
2. Adam Gilchrist has captained Australia in Test cricket: agree or disagree?
3. Which is a form of dance: Tango or Tutu?

4. The health benefits and distinctive yellow colour of which spice come principally from a substance called curcumin?
5. Harpy, golden, bald and sea are different species of which bird?
6. Which four-letter name would you place before Pratap and after Jaspal?
7. What is the word?

Set 4

1. Which mythological character's name means 'Rama with an axe': Parashurama or Balaram?
2. Which continent has been called 'the Oldest Continent,' 'the Last of Lands,' and 'the Last Frontier'?
3. Who is the director of *Munnabhai MBBS*: Vidhu Vinod Chopra or Rajkumar Hirani?
4. Which of these animals can be found only on the island of Madagascar: aye-aye or aardvark?
5. Who is the spiritual head of the Tibetan Buddhists?
6. If you were facing north, which direction would your right hand point towards?
7. What is the word?

Set 5

1. Which moon would you find in the flag of Pakistan: crescent moon or full moon?
2. Which brother of Kishore Kumar worked as a lab assistant in Bombay Talkies?
3. In Maharashtra, which town is the site of Pandu and Chamar cave temples: Nasik or Ajanta?
4. Sirius, the brightest star in the night sky, is also called

the Cat Star or Dog Star?

5. Give me a six-letter word for a traditional story popularly regarded as historical but not authenticated.
6. Till 1990, Germany was divided into West Germany and which other part?
7. What is the word?

MATHS AND IQ

1. Why should a detective disbelieve this story? The spy entered the room, switched on the light, took a book from the shelf, and placed the secret note between pages 19 and 20.
2. Would it be cheaper to take one friend to the movies twice, or two friends at the same time?
3. Fill in the blanks with either addition, subtraction, multiplication or division to figure out the correct answer. Go sequentially from left to right without following BODMAS.

8		8		26		15	=	6

4. Which number comes next in the series: 3, 8, 15, 24, 35,____?
5. Fill in the blanks with either addition, subtraction, multiplication or division to figure out the correct answer. Go sequentially from left to right without following BODMAS.

4		3		30		14	=	15

VOCABULARY

1. Rearrange the letters of the word 'FALSE' to find the name of some insects.
2. Rearrange the letters of the word 'SINK' to get a body organ.
3. Rearrange the letters of the word 'LAST' to find a compound of sodium.
4. Read the word 'SORE' to get the Greek god of love.
5. Read the word 'REPAID' backwards to get a baby's underpants.

SPEED

1. What fungus do bakers use?
2. Along the banks of which river is Agra located?
3. The word 'nasal' would describe which part of your body?
4. In cricket, how many runs are scored if a six is hit from a no ball?
5. Which of Batman's friends sound like a bird?
6. Besides Indira Gandhi, name another woman prime minister of India.
7. A stallion is a male horse: serious or joking?
8. Which is taller: the Qutb Minar or Charminar?
9. Who became the king of Kishkindha immediately after Bali's death?
10. Which key on a computer keyboard sounds like you have changed position?

ANSWERS

TAKE YOUR PICK

1. Khaki
2. Gandhari
3. Leo Tolstoy
4. Assam
5. Grapes
6. *Gulliver's Travels*
7. Odissi
8. Attorney General
9. Best Editing
10. Lions

WHAT'S THE QUESTION

1. What is dirham?
2. What is the French national anthem called?
3. In which ship did Francis Drake sail around the world?
4. What is the French equivalent of 'thank you very much'?
5. What is the Big Bang theory?
6. Name one of Spider-Man's enemies.
7. What is the human version of Mad Cow Disease called?
8. Name a famous book on films written by Satyajit Ray.

9. Name a famous painting by Pablo Picasso.
10. In cricket, what is full toss?

MIXED BAG

1. Wellington
2. Ravana
3. Liger
4. *Les Misérables*
5. India Gate
6. M.S. Subbulakshmi
7. Slavery
8. Neptune
9. *The Ten Commandments*
10. Fish

SPOT THE ANSWER

1. Have a prosperous and happy new year
2. Dhyan Chand's birthday. He was one of the greatest hockey players of all times.
3. To be licked. It is a Latin word.
4. They generally hunt at night.
5. Cook in it (Chinese cooking vessel)

CONFIDENCE ROUND

1. Moon
2. Six
3. Harishchandra
4. Tin

5. Joking
6. Mohammad Kaif
7. Iguana
8. Rockies
9. Organization
10. Cochin

WHAT'S THE WORD

Set 1
1. Daffodil
2. India
3. Mahabharata
4. Paris
5. Long John Silver
6. Eskimo
7. DIMPLE

Set 2
1. Monkey
2. Agree
3. Rani Mukherjee
4. Brahmaputra
5. Lakshmana
6. Eiffel Tower
7. MARBLE

Set 3
1. Mali
2. Agree
3. Tango

4. Turmeric
5. Eagle
6. Rana
7. MATTER

Set 4

1. Parashurama
2. Australia
3. Rajkumar Hirani
4. Aye-aye
5. Dalai Lama
6. East
7. PARADE

Set 5

1. Crescent moon
2. Ashok Kumar
3. Nasik
4. Dog Star
5. Legend
6. East Germany
7. CANDLE

MATHS AND IQ

1. In any book, pages 19 and 20 are two sides of the same page.
2. Two friends at the same time
3. | 8 | Multiply | 8 | Plus | 26 | Divide | 15 | = | 6 |
4. 48 (Odd numbers from 5 onwards are added to get the next number.)

5. | 4 | Plus | 3 | Multiply | 30 | Divide | 14 | = | 15 |

VOCABULARY

1. FLEAS
2. SKIN
3. SALT
4. EROS
5. DIAPER

SPEED

1. Yeast
2. Yamuna
3. The nose
4. Seven
5. Robin
6. There are none.
7. Serious
8. The Qutb Minar
9. Sugriva
10. Shift

SET 10

TAKE YOUR PICK

1. In the hermitage of which sage was Shakuntala brought up?
   a. Kanva
   b. Agastya
   c. Dronacharya

2. According to Thomas Alva Edison, what was 1 per cent inspiration and 99 per cent perspiration?
   a. Genius
   b. Happiness
   c. His phonograph

3. Which leader did Mahatma Gandhi call the 'Prince among Patriots'?
   a. Netaji Subhas Chandra Bose
   b. Jawaharlal Nehru
   c. Vallabhbhai Patel

4. If you were a cartographer, what would you be studying?
   a. Maps
   b. Coins
   c. Postcards

5. Which nut is attached to a yellow or red pear-shaped false fruit?
   a. Almond
   b. Cashew nut
   c. Walnut

6. Which country's population consists mostly of Flemings and Walloons?
   a. Denmark
   b. Belgium
   c. Paraguay

7. In literature, which author used the pseudonym Isaac Bickerstaff?
   a. Mark Twain
   b. Jonathan Swift
   c. Roald Dahl

8. With which dance form would you associate the famous dancers Rukmini Devi Arundale and Yamini Krishnamurthy?
   a. Kathak
   b. Manipuri
   c. Bharatnatyam

9. Who appoints the Attorney General of India?
   a. The president
   b. The prime minister
   c. The chief justice of the Supreme Court

10. In 2008, who became the first Indian actor to receive the prestigious Malaysian title, 'Datuk'?

a. Aamir Khan
b. Ajay Devgn
c. Shah Rukh Khan

WHAT'S THE QUESTION

1. *With Malice towards One and All*
2. This Indian freedom fighter transformed Ganesha Chaturthi into a public event in Maharashtra.
3. Haradanahalli
4. Albert Mission School, Vinayak Mudali Street and Lawley Extension
5. The All England Lawn Tennis and Croquet Club
6. He played the role of Dennis the Menace in the 1993 film of the same name.
7. He created raga Priyadarshini in Indira Gandhi's honour.
8. Barchans
9. Chingachgook and his son Uncas
10. Epsilon, Theta, Iota, Sigma and Pi

MIXED BAG

1. Which social networking site was acquired by Facebook when it had just thirteen employees?
2. K2 or Godwin Austen is the world's second highest peak. To which range of mountains does it belong?
3. The Indian name of this snake is ajgar. What is its English name?
4. In 1985, who became the first unseeded player to win the Wimbledon Men's Singles tournament?

5. Which two words are inscribed below the abacus on the Emblem of India?
6. Name the German businessman who saved more than 1,000 Jews from Nazi camps and has been immortalized in an award-winning film?
7. Liquefied Petroleum Gas (LPG) is chemically odourless. Yet whenever this cooking gas leaks, we can smell it. Why?
8. Which infamous prison would you associate with 14 July 1789?
9. What is common to the following: banganapalli, safeda, langra, chausa and malda?
10. Fill in the missing word in these lines from a poem by Nissim Ezekiel: 'Thank God the _____ picked on me/ And spared my children.'

SPOT THE ANSWER

1. How did Ranjit Singh lose one of his eyes?
    a. Injury while playing polo
    b. Born with one eye
    c. Due to smallpox

2. Prince Philip is the president emeritus of which of these organisations?
    a. World Wildlife Fund
    b. World Wrestling Federation
    c. World Whale Foundation

3. Which collection of stories is also called *Alf laylah wa laylah*?

a. *Arabian Nights*
b. *Jataka Tales*
c. *Panchatantra*

4. Who was the king of Japan during World War II?
    a. Ajinomoto
    b. Hirohito
    c. Akihito

5. The dog that would eventually evolve into Mickey Mouse's dog Pluto made his debut in The Chain Gang as a...
    a. Dachshund
    b. Mixed breed
    c. Bloodhound

CONFIDENCE ROUND

1. What would ache if you had a migraine?
2. What is pressed while changing gears: clutch or brake?
3. Abhimanyu was the son of Subhadra and which Pandava?
4. Blue, Green and Congo are different species of which bird: peacock or parrot?
5. Which of these rivers flows into the Bay of Bengal: Narmada or Godavari?
6. In Rudyard Kipling's *The Jungle Book*, what kind of a creature was Baloo?
7. With which letter do the names of most films directed by Rakesh Roshan start: 'K' or 'R'?
8. The official residence of the prime minister of India is

in New Delhi or Mumbai?
9. The name of which Olympic sport comes from a Latin word meaning 'belonging to a horseman'?
10. Which of these is chiefly used to make platinum alloys: iridium or radium?

WHAT'S THE WORD

Set 1

1. Gases that heat up the atmosphere by trapping sunlight are called greenhouse gases or redhouse gases?
2. Which dance form originated in eastern India: Odissi or Kathak?
3. In Scotland, what kind of a water body is a 'loch': sea or lake?
4. What was the name of a system of ethics founded by Akbar: *Din-i-Ilahi* or *Baburnama*?
5. Which actress is the sister of Ahana and the step sister of actor Bobby Deol?
6. Auckland is the largest urban area of which island nation?
7. What is the word?

Set 2

1. Raja Ravi Varma was a famous actor or painter?
2. Another term used for a lift is an escalator or an elevator?
3. Which of these is an Indian sweetmeat: rasmalai or rasam?
4. If P stands for Postal and N stands for Number, what

does 'I' in PIN stand for: India or Index?
5. Which famous leader was born in Cuttack on 23 January 1897?
6. In which north Indian state would you be if you were sightseeing in Dalhousie?
7. What's the word?

Set 3

1. Who was the successor to Chandragupta I, the ruler of the Gupta empire?
2. Which state capital comes administratively under Papum Pare district: Itanagar or Kohima?
3. Rajapuri, langra and dussehri are some of the varieties of which fruit?
4. Till date, which country has won the ICC Cricket World Cup only once: West Indies or Pakistan?
5. Hindu mythology portrays goddess Saraswati as being seated on which flower?
6. The name of which currency was chosen by the European Council meeting in Madrid in 1995?
7. What is the word?

Set 4

1. The sun is a star or a planet?
2. Which snake kills its victims using venom: cobra or python?
3. Sourav Ganguly is a left-handed or a right-handed bowler?
4. Amitabh Bachchan made his debut as an actor in *Saat Hindustani*: agree or disagree?
5. The name of which fruit comes from the Greek word

for 'large melon'?
6. Which eleven-letter word ending in 'ware' describes pots and dishes made of baked clay?
7. What is the word?

Set 5

1. Name Ralf Schumacher's brother who also competed in the same sport.
2. No two giraffes have the same pattern of spots: agree or disagree?
3. In the Ramayana, who was Kusha's mother?
4. Which of its world heritage sites does India share with Bangladesh: Sunderbans or Kaziranga National Park?
5. Who is the famous paternal grandmother of Rahul Gandhi?
6. F is the symbol of which chemical element?
7. What is the word?

MATHS AND IQ

1. A test has twenty questions. If Peter gets 80 per cent correct, how many did he miss?
2. Fill in the blanks with either addition, subtraction, multiplication or division to figure out the correct answer. Go sequentially from left to right without following BODMAS.

| 21 | | 7 | | 10 | | 2 | = | 11 |

3. A zoo had 44 female and 36 male zebras. Which is the correct ratio of females to males?
4. Which number comes next in the series: 1, 1, 2, 3, 4, 9, 8, _____

5. Fill in the blanks with either addition, subtraction, multiplication or division to figure out the correct answer. Go sequentially from left to right without following BODMAS.

84		47		2		3	=	13

VOCABULARY

1. Rearrange the letters of the word 'TASTE' to find what Uttarakhand is.
2. Rearrange the letters of the word 'MARY' to find one of the wings of the armed forces.
3. Rearrange the letters of the word 'WENT' to find the name of an amphibian.
4. Read the word 'FLOG' backwards to get the name of a game.
5. Read the word 'MADE' backwards to get a town in Holland or hard cheese.

SPEED

1. What is the study or collection of coins, paper currency and medals called?
2. Who was the first American to go to space: Neil Armstrong or Alan Shepard?
3. On which part of your body might you wear pumps?
4. Who was president of the US immediately before Bill Clinton?
5. Workers are the only bees that most people ever see: serious or joking?
6. Which country hosted the 2000 Olympic Games?

7. How many sides does a heptagon have?
8. Which geometric instrument is used to draw arcs and circles?
9. The Hawaii Islands are a part of which country?
10. In *Raja Hindustani*, who played the role of the Aarti Sehgal?

ANSWERS

TAKE YOUR PICK

1. Kanva
2. Genius
3. Netaji Subhas Chandra Bose
4. Maps
5. Cashew nut
6. Belgium
7. Jonathan Swift
8. Bharatnatyam
9. The president
10. Shah Rukh Khan

WHAT'S THE QUESTION

1. What was the name of the popular column written by Khushwant Singh?
2. Who was Lokmanya Tilak?
3. What is the first name of Prime Minister Deve Gowda?
4. Name some famous landmarks in Malgudi, the fictional town created by R.K. Narayan.
5. What is the full name of the club that owns and governs the Wimbledon tennis tournament?
6. Who is Mason Gamble?
7. Who is Amjad Ali Khan?
8. What is a crescent-shaped sand dune called?

9. In the book of the same name, who were the last of the Mohicans?
10. Name some of the letters of the Greek alphabet.

MIXED BAG

1. Instagram
2. Karakoram
3. Python
4. Boris Becker
5. *Satyameva Jayate*
6. Oskar Schindler
7. The smell is deliberately added so that people can detect leaks.
8. Bastille
9. All of them are varieties of mangoes.
10. Scorpion

SPOT THE ANSWER

1. Due to smallpox
2. World Wildlife Fund
3. *Arabian Nights*
4. Hirohito
5. Bloodhound

CONFIDENCE ROUND

1. Your head
2. Clutch
3. Arjuna

4. Peacock
5. Godavari
6. Black bear
7. 'K'
8. New Delhi
9. Equestrian
10. Iridium

WHAT'S THE WORD

Set 1

1. Greenhouse gases
2. Odissi
3. Lake
4. *Din-i-Ilahi*
5. Esha Deol
6. New Zealand
7. GOLDEN

Set 2

1. Painter
2. Elevator
3. Rasmalai
4. Index
5. Subhas Chandra Bose
6. Himachal Pradesh
7. PERISH

Set 3

1. Samudragupta
2. Itanagar

3. Mango
4. Pakistan
5. Lotus
6. Euro
7. SIMPLE

Set 4

1. Star
2. Cobra
3. Right-handed
4. Agree
5. Pumpkin
6. Earthenware
7. SCRAPE

Set 5

1. Michael Schumacher
2. Agree
3. Sita
4. Sunderbans
5. Indira Gandhi
6. Fluorine
7. MASSIF

MATHS AND IQ

1. Four
2. | 21 | Divide | 7 | Plus | 10 | Minus | 2 | = | 11 |
3. 11:9
4. 27 (Two consecutive series are present. In the first series, each number is multiplied by 2 and in the

second, by 3.)

5. | 84 | Minus | 47 | Plus | 2 | Divide | 3 | = | 13 |

VOCABULARY

1. STATE
2. ARMY
3. NEWT
4. GOLF
5. EDAM

SPEED

1. Numismatics
2. Alan Shepard
3. Feet. It is a type of shoe.
4. George H.W. Bush
5. Serious
6. Australia
7. Seven
8. Compass
9. The US
10. Karishma Kapoor

SET 11

TAKE YOUR PICK

1. In the Mahabharata, who was Nakula's mother?
   a. Kunti
   b. Madri
   c. Gandhari

2. Which element's chemical symbol Au derives from the Latin *aurum*, for Aurora the goddess of dawn?
   a. Silver
   b. Gold
   c. Platinum

3. For which monument were 20,000 workmen accommodated in a small town named Mumtazabad in the 1630s?
   a. Red Fort
   b. Taj Mahal
   c. Agra Fort

4. In 1917, 1944 and 1963, which organization had the unique distinction of being awarded the Nobel Peace Prize?
   a. Grameen Bank
   b. United Nations Children's Fund (UNICEF)
   c. The International Committee of the Red Cross

5. Akoori is a traditional dish of which community?
   a. Buddhists
   b. Parsis
   c. Jains

6. Which mountain range is divided into the Sambhar–Sirohi range and the Sambhar–Khetri range?
   a. Aravalli
   b. Satpura
   c. Himalayas

7. With which embroidery would you associate 'Tota Bagh', 'Bawan Bagh' and 'Ashrafi Bagh'?
   a. Kantha
   b. Chikankari
   c. Phulkari

8. Kamban, Krittibas and Tulsidas have all written different versions of which work?
   a. Ramayana
   b. Vedas
   c. Mahabharata

9. Who served as the prime minister of India for about seventeen years?
   a. Jawaharlal Nehru
   b. Indira Gandhi
   c. P.V. Narasimha Rao

10. Who directed the 2005 film *Iqbal*?
    a. Nagesh Kukunoor

b. Mohit Suri
c. Meera Nair

WHAT'S THE QUESTION

1. It was the first month of the early Roman calendar.
2. It comprised one big Oscar and seven little ones.
3. The fabric calico is named after a city in this state of India.
4. In the Ramayana, he was Shatrughna's father.
5. He wrote *Our Trees Still Grow in Dehra*.
6. Nadir Shah gave its name
7. *Moonwalk* (book)
8. Changi Airport
9. Kyats
10. William the Conqueror defeated King Harold II of England

MIXED BAG

1. In 1930, who started the Vanar Sena, a children's brigade to help freedom fighters?
2. It is one of the largest Indian antelopes. The male of the species has a smooth bluish-grey coat and is also called 'blue bull'. How is it commonly known in India?
3. Which Indian emulated Bob Massie's feat of sixteen wickets on Test debut?
4. What would you associate with 'going under the hammer'?
5. Which historically important structure of the Mughals is also known as 'Fort Rouge' or 'Qila-i-Akbari'?

6. Which term, also meaning 'to fix firmly and deeply in a surrounding mass', was used to describe journalists who travelled with allied army formations during the Gulf War of 2003?
7. The Bronx, Brooklyn, Queens, Staten Island and Manhattan together form which city?
8. If you had excess bilirubin in your bloodstream, what would you be suffering from?
9. Name the American president and his wife who acted in the 1957 film Hellcats of the Navy.
10. Which Mughal emperor planted 1,00,000 mango trees in Darbhanga, Bihar at a place now known as Lakhi Bagh?

SPOT THE ANSWER

1. Who had four sons named Harilal, Manilal, Ramdas and Devdas?
   a. Subhas Chandra Bose
   b. Bhagat Singh
   c. Mahatma Gandhi

2. The Danjon scale, ranging from L=0 (meaning very dark) to L=4 (meaning very bright copper red to orange), measures the brightness of which phenomenon?
   a. Lunar eclipse
   b. Aurora Borealis
   c. Rainbow

3. In Japan, what would you do with a kimono?

a. Wear it
   b. Eat it
   c. Write with it

4. Noshak is the highest point of which country?
   a. Pakistan
   b. China
   c. Afghanistan

5. How did espresso coffee get its name?
   a. A variation of the word 'express'
   b. From the word 'espressino', meaning cold coffee
   c. From the Italian word for 'pressed out'

CONFIDENCE ROUND

1. Which famous astrologer was born in 1503 and died in 1566?
2. In Hinduism, swarg is heaven or hell?
3. Some owls are also active during the day: serious or joking?
4. Complete the title of this Hindi film: *Jo Jeeta Wohi*_____
5. What is the shape of the balls used in the Adelaide Oval?
6. In the works by Agatha Christie, what was Miss Marple's first name?
7. Mg is the symbol of which chemical element: manganese or magnesium?
8. Which of these rivers flows through the states of Karnataka and Tamil Nadu: Cauvery or Narmada?

9. Which fruit, rich in papain, an enzyme present in its milky juice, is normally used to make meat tender?
10. A pentathlon has five, ten or fifteen events?

WHAT'S THE WORD

Set 1

1. Who is the first Indian woman to scale the summit of Mount Everest?
2. In which Indian state is the Manas Wildlife Sanctuary?
3. Which Indian said, 'Wars cannot be won by bullets, but only by bleeding hearts'?
4. Which was Anna Sewell's only published novel?
5. What is defined in the dictionary as 'a report, especially in a newspaper, which gives the news of someone's death and details about their life'?
6. How many fish would you have if you had one cod, three jellyfish and four crayfish?
7. What's the word?

Set 2

1. Which emperor was the great grandfather of Aurangzeb?
2. Which Indian state was previously called the United Provinces?
3. What colour does blue litmus paper turn into when put in acid?
4. Which novel by Charles Dickens is subtitled *The Parish Boy's Progress*?
5. Which narrow bones form the cage around your heart and lungs?

6. In the place of which common word would you use an ampersand?
7. What's the word?

Set 3

1. Cirrus, cirrocumulus, stratus and nimbostratus are types of what?
2. What is the name of the first Asterix book?
3. Which musical instrument was referred to as Shata-Tantri Veena in ancient times?
4. According to mythology, who lifted the Govardhana mountain?
5. Think logically! Which planet was the first to be explored by man?
6. What don't manx cats and humans have, that most monkeys do?
7. What's the word?

Set 4

1. Barking, swamp, musk and rein are all types of which animal?
2. The leaves of which tree appear on the flag of the United Nations?
3. Which word meaning a short official note, memorandum, or voucher, typically recording a sum owed comes from a Hindi word meaning 'note, pass'?
4. Which sport was originally known as *jeu de paumme* in French meaning the game of the palm?
5. Which city in the United Kingdom is known as the 'City of Spires' for its Gothic towers and steeples:

Glasgow or Oxford?
6. *Oryza sativa* is the scientific name of which food grain?
7. What's the word?

Set 5

1. Which Mughal emperor was born at Umarkot in 1542?
2. Name the largest species of rat found in India. (Hint: In Telugu, it is called *pandi-kokku*.)
3. Popeye has an anchor tattooed on his arm. What tattoo do his four nephews have?
4. In India, which embroidery uses white yarn on colourless muslins called *tanzeb*?
5. Which planet was discovered by astronomer William Herschel?
6. Of which music group are Pakistan-based Bilal Maqsood and Faisal Kapadia members?
7. What's the word?

MATHS AND IQ

1. How is my father's only sister's paternal grandfather's only grandson related to me?
2. Fill in the blanks with either addition, subtraction, multiplication or division to figure out the correct answer. Go sequentially from left to right without following BODMAS.

| 23 | | 14 | | 15 | | 2 | = | 11 |

3. In a certain code, if MONITOR is written as OMPGVMT, how is CURSOR written?
4. Which number will logically complete the sequence?

7, 12, 22, 37, 57, ____

5. Fill in the blanks with either addition, subtraction, multiplication or division to figure out the correct answer. Go sequentially from left to right without following BODMAS.

| 43 | | 10 | | 3 | | 2 | = | 13 |

VOCABULARY

1. Rearrange the letters of the word 'DEAR' to get what you do when you open a book.
2. Rearrange the letters of the word 'PLANE' to get an Asian country.
3. Rearrange the letters of the word 'LEAK' to get a water body.
4. Read the word 'LAGER' backwards to get a word meaning 'royal'.
5. Read the word 'BAT' backwards to get a computer key or small flap.

SPEED

1. Which story by Louisa May Alcott is about four sisters: Meg, Jo, Beth and Amy?
2. In World War II, what was the US's M-4 General Sherman?
3. On which part of the body are mittens worn?
4. Over 70 per cent of the population of greater one-horned rhinos occurs in which national park?
5. Think differently! Which part of a mechanical watch sounds like it had a previous owner?

6. Nippon or Nihon is another name for which country?
7. What makes up 99.8 per cent of the mass of the entire solar system?
8. Who became the president of Argentina after the death of Juan Perón in 1974?
9. In Chinese, the name of which food item literally means 'stir-fried' noodles?
10. On which famous street is the New York Stock Exchange located?

ANSWERS

TAKE YOUR PICK

1. Madri
2. Gold
3. Taj Mahal
4. The International Committee of the Red Cross
5. Parsis
6. Aravalli
7. Phulkari
8. Ramayana
9. Jawaharlal Nehru
10. Nagesh Kukunoor

WHAT'S THE QUESTION

1. What is March?
2. What was unusual about the Oscar presented to Walt Disney for *Snow White and the Seven Dwarfs*?
3. What is Kerala?
4. Who was Dasharatha?
5. Name a book by Ruskin Bond.
6. Who gave the Koh-i-noor diamond its name?
7. What is the title of Michael Jackson's autobiography?
8. What is the name of Singapore's airport?
9. What is the currency of Myanmar (formerly Burma)?
10. Who defeated who at the Battle of Hastings (1066 CE)?

MIXED BAG

1. Indira Gandhi
2. Nilgai
3. Narendra Hirwani
4. Going to be sold at an auction
5. Agra Fort
6. Embed
7. New York City
8. Jaundice
9. Ronald and Nancy Reagan
10. Akbar

SPOT THE ANSWER

1. Mahatma Gandhi
2. Lunar eclipse
3. Wear it
4. Afghanistan
5. From the Italian word for 'pressed out'

CONFIDENCE ROUND

1. Nostradamus
2. Heaven
3. Serious
4. *Sikander*
5. Round
6. Jane
7. Magnesium
8. Cauvery

9. Papaya
10. Five

WHAT'S THE WORD

Set 1

1. Bachendri Pal
2. Assam
3. Mahatma Gandhi
4. *Black Beauty*
5. Obituary
6. One. Cod is a fish. Jellyfish and crayfish are not fish.
7. BAMBOO

Set 2

1. Akbar
2. Uttar Pradesh
3. Red
4. *Oliver Twist*
5. Ribs
6. And
7. AURORA

Set 3

1. Clouds
2. *Asterix the Gaul*
3. Santoor
4. Krishna
5. Earth
6. Tails
7. CASKET

Set 4

1. Deer
2. Olive
3. Chit
4. Tennis
5. Oxford
6. Rice
7. DOCTOR

Set 5

1. Akbar
2. Bandicoot
3. Anchors as well
4. *Chikankari*
5. Uranus
6. Strings
7. ABACUS

MATHS AND IQ

1. My father
2. | 23 | Plus | 14 | Minus | 15 | Divided | 2 | = | 11 |
3. ESTQQP
4. 82 (7+5=12, 12+10=22, 22+15=37, 37+20=57, 57+25=82)
5. | 43 | Minus | 10 | Divided | 3 | Plus | 2 | = | 13 |

VOCABULARY

1. READ

2. NEPAL
3. LAKE
4. REGAL
5. TAB

SPEED

1. *Little Women*
2. A tank
3. Hands
4. Kaziranga National Park
5. The second hand
6. Japan
7. The sun
8. Isabel Perón
9. Chow Mein
10. Wall Street

SET 12

TAKE YOUR PICK

1. Who became Uttara's dance and music teacher at Raja Virata's court?
   a. Arjuna
   b. Bhima
   c. Sahadeva

2. The name of which shiny mineral means 'crumb' in Latin?
   a. Silver
   b. Mica
   c. Platinum

3. Which of these was the principal seat of authority of the Chandela rulers?
   a. Khajuraho
   b. Mahabalipuram
   c. Hampi

4. Which of these spices is produced by treating the crimson stigma of a flower?
   a. Mace
   b. Turmeric
   c. Saffron

5. In his travelogue, which island did Marco Polo refer to as the 'Female Island'?
   a. Minicoy
   b. Little Andaman
   c. Great Nicobar

6. In the abbreviation ATM, what does 'M' stand for?
   a. Machine
   b. Mobile
   c. Money

7. Who invited Atomba Singh to teach Manipuri dancing in Bengal in the 1920s?
   a. Mahatma Gandhi
   b. Rabindranath Tagore
   c. Subhas Chandra Bose

8. In 2002, a dinosaur was named in honour of which famous science fiction author?
   a. Arthur C. Clarke
   b. Stephen King
   c. Michael Crichton

9. From 1977 to 1979, Atal Bihari Vajpayee was Union cabinet minister of…
   a. Information and Broadcasting
   b. External Affairs
   c. Civil Aviation

10. In 1896, what took place for the first time in India at Watson's Hotel in Mumbai?

a. First Congress annual session
b. First film screening
c. First Filmfare Awards

WHAT'S THE QUESTION

1. JFK International Airport
2. Florence Nightingale played an important role in this war from 1853-1856.
3. *Pride and Prejudice* is one of her most famous novels.
4. Ringgit
5. Taming the ferocious horses of Diomedes and overcoming the Nemaean lion.
6. They are the only mammal capable of true flight.
7. He married Dimple Kapadia in 1973.
8. In *Asterix* comics, he fell into a cauldron of magic potion when he was a little boy.
9. Ophiuchus
10. She is Lava and Kusha's mother.

MIXED BAG

1. Tanzania was formed by the merger of which two sovereign states?
2. Sarojini Naidu was the governor of UP. Name her daughter, who became the governor of West Bengal.
3. A species of which member of the weasel family is called 'fisi maji,' meaning water hyena in Swahili?
4. Traditionally, which famous sporting event is associated with strawberries and cream?
5. Robert Clive fought Siraj-ud-Daula in the Battle of

Plassey in 1757. In which present-day Indian state is Plassey located?

6. Which word connects the repetition of sound caused by the reflection of sound waves and a code word representing the letter E, used in radio communication?
7. Which is the senior-most regiment in the Indian Army?
8. I am a nine-letter word. My first letter is the Roman letter for 100. The next three are a zodiac sign and the last two are the name of the Egyptian Sun God. Who am I?
9. Name the antibiotic also known as the first 'wonder drug'.
10. Which crime fighter's parents were killed by Joe 'Chill' Chilton?

SPOT THE ANSWER

1. With reference to the World Wide Web, what does the term 'hit rate' refer to?
   a. Cricket scores on the net
   b. Being hit by a virus
   c. The number of visitors to a website

2. In Hindi films, Begum Mumtaz Jehan Dehlavi was the original name of which actress?
   a. Madhubala
   b. Meena Kumari
   c. Waheeda Rahman

3. In 2006, which country slapped a 5 per cent tax on chopsticks over concerns of deforestation?
   a. Egypt
   b. Korea
   c. China

4. Why do bees perform a complicated movement called the 'waggle dance'?
   a. To teach young bees to fly
   b. To tell other bees where to find food
   c. To warn bees from other hives

5. Who sang 'The Song for Peace' minutes before he was assassinated?
   a. John F. Kennedy
   b. Abraham Lincoln
   c. Yitzhak Rabin

CONFIDENCE ROUND

1. Which Italian city has a famous leaning tower?
2. Which scientist coined the name 'oxygen'?
3. Which term relates to horses: equine or porcine?
4. The Nag river flows by Nagpur: serious or joking?
5. Shah Shuja and Aurangzeb were the sons of which Mughal emperor: Shah Jahan or Jahangir?
6. In comics, Popeye and Brutus compete with each other for whose affection?
7. The Ranji Trophy was named after which former cricketer?
8. What would a Chinese individual do with a won ton?

9. How is Rahul Gandhi related to Feroze Varun Gandhi?
10. What does 'I' in FBI stand for: Intelligence or Investigation?

WHAT'S THE WORD

Set 1

1. Which vehicle was originally a mobile temporary hospital that followed the army from place to place?
2. Which of these is often called the unicorns of the sea: Narwhal or Beluga?
3. What is nearly equal to 2.54 cm: an inch or a foot?
4. After which famous historical leader is the capital of Gujarat named?
5. Spanning seven countries, which is the longest continental mountain range in the world?
6. The name of which popular board game for two to four players comes from the Latin word meaning 'I play'?
7. What's the word?

Set 2

1. Siamese, Persian, Caffre and Sphynx are all types of which animal?
2. Which unit of weight is one-sixteenth of a pound: gram or ounce?
3. In India, which monument is seen on the reverse side of the ₹50 note?
4. Red is a primary colour or a secondary colour?
5. In which continent is Spain located?

6. On a Scrabble board, the score for an entire word is tripled when one of its letters is placed on a square of which colour?
7. What's the word?

Set 3

1. Name the Chinese pilgrim who came to India during the reign of Chandragupta II.
2. What are Basmati and Manipuri different varieties of: roti or rice?
3. Other than India, which Asian country begins with the letters 'Ind' and ends with 'ia'?
4. Which caves have been excavated out of the vertical face of Charanandri Hills?
5. The inability of which gas to support life led Antoine-Laurent Lavoisier to name it 'azote'?
6. Name the most well-known extinct flightless bird of Mauritius.
7. What's the word?

Set 4

1. What is the colour of emerald?
2. Muhi-al-Din Muhammad was the original name of which great Mughal emperor?
3. Which lake in India shares its name with the Hindi name of pulses?
4. If 'Big Bird' is the nickname for cricketer Joel Garner, then which footballer was nicknamed the 'Little Bird'?
5. Which Greek nymph's hopeless love for Narcissus made her fade away until only her voice remained?
6. Who was raised by the apes: Mowgli or Tarzan?

7. What's the word?

Set 5

1. Which of these is an amphibian: frog or turtle?
2. In the world of music, what would you associate with Shellac, Vulcanite, Columbia, Edison Diamond and Vinyl?
3. In India, if a woman can vote at the age of eighteen, at what minimum age can a man vote?
4. Is Ooty in the Nilgiris or Aravallis?
5. The Latin name for which metal is *cuprum*?
6. In India, how is a flag flown when there is a state mourning: full mast or half mast?
7. What's the word?

MATHS AND IQ

1. In a class, Indumati's rank is 12th from the top and 32nd from the bottom. How many students are there in the class?
2. Fill in the blanks with either addition, subtraction, multiplication or division to figure out the correct answer. Go sequentially from left to right without following BODMAS.

| 25 | | 3 | | 16 | | 7 | = | 13 |

3. Which set of letters will logically follow the pattern ZIFZY, IFZYZ, FZYZI, _____
4. Fill in the blanks with either addition, subtraction, multiplication or division to figure out the correct answer. Go sequentially from left to right without following BODMAS.

| 7 | | 4 | | 27 | | 5 | = | 11 |

5. If you add all the dots on a dice, except 4, which number would you get?

VOCABULARY

1. Rearrange the letters of the word 'LATE' to get a word that means story.
2. Rearrange the letters of the word 'SAVE' to get an object you might put flowers in.
3. Rearrange the letters of the word 'LEAST' to get a word that means 'to take something illegally or without permission'.
4. Read the word 'PART' backwards to get a device to catch animals.
5. Read the word 'LIAR' backwards to get what trains run on.

SPEED

1. In 1325, Prince Jauna became ruler under which name?
2. What constitutes more than 50 per cent of a dried date, in terms of weight?
3. Which is the only even prime number?
4. Which organ in the human body is the word 'pulmonary' connected with?
5. In which sport were Misha Grewal and Bhuvaneshwari Kumari women's national champions?
6. A camel's stomach is divided into how many chambers?

7. Who was the first Indian to receive both the Nobel Prize and the Bharat Ratna?
8. Which desert covers almost all of Botswana?
9. Which musical instrument is also known as venu, vamsi, murali, pillankarovi and kolalu?
10. Which planet was named by the Romans after their god of war because of its red, blood-like colour?

ANSWERS

TAKE YOUR PICK

1. Arjuna
2. Mica
3. Khajuraho. It is a village in Madhya Pradesh.
4. Saffron
5. Minicoy
6. Machine (ATM = Automated Teller Machine)
7. Rabindranath Tagore
8. Michael Crichton
9. External Affairs
10. First film screening

WHAT'S THE QUESTION

1. What was the Idlewild Airport renamed as in 1963?
2. What is the Crimean War?
3. Who is Jane Austen?
4. What is the currency of Malaysia?
5. Name any two of Hercules' Twelve Labours.
6. What are bats?
7. Who was Rajesh Khanna?
8. Who is Obelix?
9. What is sometimes called the thirteenth sign of the zodiac?
10. Who is Sita?

MIXED BAG
1. Tanganyika and Zanzibar
2. Padmaja Naidu
3. Otter
4. Wimbledon Tennis Championships
5. West Bengal
6. Echo
7. The president's bodyguard
8. Cleopatra
9. Penicillin
10. Bruce Wayne/Batman

SPOT THE ANSWER

1. The number of visitors to a website
2. Madhubala
3. China
4. To tell other bees where to find food
5. Yitzhak Rabin. He was the prime minister of Israel, and led peace negotiations with Palestine and neighbouring Arab countries.

CONFIDENCE ROUND

1. Pisa
2. Antoine Lavoisier
3. Equine
4. Serious
5. Shah Jahan
6. Olive Oyl
7. K.S. Ranjitsinhji (1872–1933), who played Test cricket

for England.
8. Eat it or cook it
9. They are cousins.
10. Investigation

WHAT'S THE WORD

Set 1
1. Ambulance
2. Narwhal
3. Inch
4. Mahatma Gandhi
5. Andes
6. Ludo
7. ANIMAL

Set 2
1. Cat
2. Ounce
3. Parliament of India
4. Primary colour
5. Europe
6. Red
7. COPPER

Set 3
1. Fa-hien
2. Rice
3. Indonesia
4. Ellora Caves
5. Nitrogen

6. Dodo
7. FRIEND

Set 4

1. Green
2. Aurangazeb
3. Dal Lake
4. Garrincha
5. Echo
6. Tarzan
7. GADGET

Set 5

1. Frog
2. Records (LPs)
3. Eighteen
4. Nilgiris
5. Copper
6. Half mast
7. FRENCH

MATHS AND IQ

1. 43 (12+31)
2. | 25 | Multiply | 3 | Plus | 16 | Divide | 7 | = | 13 |
3. ZYZIF
4. | 7 | Multiply | 4 | Plus | 27 | Divide | 5 | = | 11 |
5. 17

VOCABULARY

1. TALE
2. VASE
3. STEAL
4. TRAP
5. RAIL

SPEED

1. Muhammad bin Tughluq
2. Sugar
3. 2
4. The lungs
5. Squash
6. Three
7. C. V. Raman
8. Kalahari
9. Flute
10. Mars

SET 13

TAKE YOUR PICK

1. In the Mahabharata, Duryodhana cried like which creature when he was born?
   a. Ass
   b. Horse
   c. Elephant

2. Which equation does David Bodanis call 'the world's most famous equation' in a biography of the equation?
   a. pr^2
   b. $E=mc^2$
   c. sxt

3. Which leader said 'Every blow aimed at me is a nail in the coffin of British imperialism'?
   a. Lal Bahadur Shastri
   b. Lala Lajpat Rai
   c. Bipin Chandra Pal

4. The roads of which Indian Union Territory were based on a unique plan called 7Vs by its original planner?
   a. Puducherry
   b. Andaman and Nicobar Islands
   c. Chandigarh

5. The name of which popular flavour comes from the Spanish word for 'pod'?
   a. Vanilla
   b. Strawberry
   c. Orange

6. What is the surname of Parvati in the *Harry Potter* series of books?
   a. Patil
   b. Peter
   c. Sarawati

7. Who is the author of *Natyashastra*?
   a. Bhasa
   b. Tulsidas
   c. Bharata Muni

8. Which Nobel Laureate's autobiography is *Freedom in Exile*?
   a. Nelson Mandela
   b. Dalai Lama
   c. Aung San Suu Kyi

9. What fraction of the Rajya Sabha retires every second year?
   a. Half
   b. One-third
   c. One-fourth

10. In a famous song from the film *Shree 420*, which accessory does Raj Kapoor describe as 'Roosi'?

a. Patloon
b. Topi
c. Joota

WHAT'S THE QUESTION

1. He was appointed editor of the newspaper, *Avanti!* in 1912.
2. They were a race of one-eyed giants; one of them was Polyphemus.
3. *Goal*
4. Bram Stoker
5. UN Day
6. The only country to have an actual building on its national flag.
7. Spirit of St Louis
8. It is a word puzzle with a grid of squares and blanks.
9. 10 Downing Street
10. Nephrons are the functional units of this organ.

MIXED BAG

1. Which is the largest country in Central America, with a coastline on both the Atlantic and the Pacific Ocean?
2. Who was the first Chairman of the Rajya Sabha?
3. Only one forest is the home of the Asiatic lion. Name it.
4. Which cricketer's autobiography is titled *Beyond 10,000, My Life Story*?
5. Which famous mausoleum was called 'a teardrop on

the cheek of time' by Rabindranath Tagore?
6. Who was issued India's first pilot's licence in 1929?
7. Who was the first National Professor of independent India?
8. Which was the first country to gain independence in the new millennium (2001–02)?
9. Who was awarded the Nobel Prize 'because of his profoundly sensitive, fresh and beautiful verse, by which, with consummate skill, he has made his poetic thought, expressed in his own English words, a part of the literature of the West'?
10. Which 1992 animated film had the tagline 'Imagine if you had three wishes, three hopes, three dreams and they all could come true'?

SPOT THE ANSWER

1. What is a plectrum used for?
    a. To strum a stringed instrument
    b. To break light into various colours
    c. To safeguard electrical appliances

2. Which cartoon character is called 'Skipper Skræk' in Denmark?
    a. Tintin
    b. Asterix
    c. Popeye

3. In medieval times, a knight threw down a gauntlet to challenge someone to a duel. Which part of his attire did a gauntlet refer to?

a. The plume from his helmet
   b. His gloves
   c. His broadsword

4. Lexico was the original name for which board game?
   a. Snakes and ladders
   b. Scrabble
   c. Monopoly

5. The word 'solstice' comes from the Latin phrase meaning…
   a. A salt cellar
   b. A five-pointed star
   c. Sun stands still

CONFIDENCE ROUND

1. A chipmunk is a squirrel or a rabbit?
2. Which of these hill stations is located in Tamil Nadu: Ooty or Nainital?
3. What is the plural of Governor-General?
4. In 2001, which Australian became the youngest man to be ranked world number one in tennis?
5. The name of which Shah Rukh Khan starrer is shortened as *DDLJ*?
6. What kind of an animal was Black Beauty in the book of the same name?
7. Generally, how many wheels does a cycle rickshaw have?
8. What is Lord Krishna's panchajanya: conch shell or mace?

9. If a small circle has 360 degrees, how many degrees does a big circle have?
10. Which ruler died while leading his troops on the battlefield: Tipu Sultan or Humayun?

WHAT'S THE WORD

Set 1

1. Whose autobiography is called *The Fairy Tale of My Life*?
2. Which Pandava was also known as Dhananjaya?
3. Which is a flattened Indian bread: kalakand or naan?
4. Which cartoon character has nephews named Huey, Dewey and Louie?
5. Which Indian prime minister was born near Varanasi but died in the capital of Uzbekistan?
6. On a computer keyboard, what does 'Esc' stand for?
7. What's the word?

Set 2

1. Which book was written by Jayadeva: *Gita Govinda* or *Sur Sagar*?
2. *Olea europaea* is the scientific name of which tree?
3. In which country would you be if you spent takas?
4. Kargil is located in which Lok Sabha constituency?
5. Which channel is known as *La Manche* in French: English Channel or Dominica Channel?
6. Who is also known as the 'Tiger of Mysore'?
7. What's the word?

Set 3

1. Which month in the Gregorian calendar is named after Julius Caesar?
2. Who has served as the chief minister of Madhya Pradesh: Rabri Devi or Uma Bharti?
3. Triton is the largest satellite of which planet?
4. Panaji is the capital of which state of India?
5. The largest variety of which creature is the Komodo Dragon?
6. The Euro symbol is inspired by which Greek letter?
7. What's the word?

Set 4

1. Which state shares a border with Jharkhand: Bihar or Haryana?
2. Which actor is sometimes referred to as Khiladi Kumar?
3. Which famous South African leader is popularly known as Madiba?
4. In terms of average elevation, which is the highest continent in the world?
5. In war parlance, which three words do you use for the stretch of ground between two enemy lines?
6. Limba Ram represented India in which sport?
7. What's the word?

Set 5

1. What would a Scotsman do with a kilt: eat it or wear it?
2. Which Greek goddess shares her name with a part of the eye?
3. Which sport did Douglas Jardine play for England?

4. Which actress is married to Ajay Devgn?
5. What would you call the official residence of an ambassador?
6. Which card is used to predict one's future: tarot card or flash card?
7. What's the word?

MATHS AND IQ

1. OBMHNMHO : PANGOLIN :: SPQUNJRF : ?
2. Fill in the blanks with either addition, subtraction, multiplication or division to figure out the correct answer. Go sequentially from left to right without following BODMAS.

19		3		14		67	=	4

3. Nalini's total bill at a restaurant was ₹84, including the waiter's tip of 5 per cent. What was the bill amount excluding the waiter's tip?
4. Joy is taller than Rishi but shorter than Rinku. Rahul is taller than Manisha but shorter than Rishi. Who is the shortest of them all?
5. Fill in the blanks with either addition, subtraction, multiplication or division to figure out the correct answer. Go sequentially from left to right without following BODMAS.

38		14		21		5	=	9

VOCABULARY

1. Rearrange the letters of the word 'NONE' to get a

colourless gas.
2. Rearrange the letters of the word 'TIMER' to get a level of excellence.
3. Rearrange the letters of the word 'AGES' to get a religious person.
4. Read the word 'DRAW' backwards to get a room in a hospital.
5. Read the word 'AVID' backward to mean a female opera singer.

SPEED

1. Which rodent gives its name to a device attached to a computer?
2. Which war ended at 11 a.m. on the eleventh day of the eleventh month in 1918?
3. What milk-based product is the main ingredient of shrikhand?
4. What important part did James Phipps play in the history of medicine?
5. Which Pandava was also known as Dharmaputra?
6. Little Miss Muffet was afraid of spiders: serious or joking?
7. How many hands does an ambidextrous man have?
8. Is the Krishna river mainly in Andhra Pradesh or Tamil Nadu?
9. Who was Kareena Kapoor's grandfather?
10. With which art form is Anjolie Ela Menon associated?

ANSWERS

TAKE YOUR PICK

1. Ass
2. $E=mc^2$
3. Lala Lajpat Rai
4. Chandigarh
5. Vanilla (The flavouring essence is derived from the pods of the vanilla orchid.)
6. Patil
7. Bharata Muni
8. Dalai Lama
9. One-third
10. Topi. The song was sung by Mukesh.

WHAT'S THE QUESTION

1. Who was Benito Mussolini?
2. Who were the Cyclopes? (singular: Cyclops)
3. Name Dhyan Chand's autobiography.
4. Who wrote *Dracula*?
5. What is 24 October celebrated as?
6. What is unique about the flag of Cambodia?
7. What was the name of Charles Lindbergh's aircraft in which he made the first solo transatlantic flight?
8. What is a crossword?
9. What is the address of the official office and residence of the prime minister of the United Kingdom?

10. What is kidney?

MIXED BAG

1. Nicaragua
2. Dr S. Radhakrishnan
3. Gir Forest in Gujarat
4. Allan Border
5. Taj Mahal
6. J.R.D. Tata
7. C. V. Raman
8. East Timor
9. Rabindranath Tagore
10. *Aladdin*

SPOT THE ANSWER

1. To strum a stringed instrument. It is a small bit of teardrop-shaped or triangular plastic.
2. Popeye
3. His gloves
4. Scrabble
5. Sun stands still

CONFIDENCE ROUND

1. Squirrel
2. Ooty
3. Governors-General
4. Lleyton Hewitt (Twenty years old)
5. *Dilwale Dulhania Le Jayenge*

6. Horse
7. Three
8. Conch shell
9. 360
10. Tipu Sultan

WHAT'S THE WORD

Set 1

1. Hans Christian Andersen
2. Arjuna
3. Naan
4. Donald Duck
5. Lal Bahadur Shastri
6. Escape
7. HANDLE

Set 2

1. *Gita Govinda*
2. Olive
3. Bangladesh
4. Ladakh
5. English Channel
6. Tipu Sultan
7. GOBLET

Set 3

1. July
2. Uma Bharti
3. Neptune
4. Goa

5. Lizard
6. Epsilon
7. JUNGLE

Set 4

1. Bihar
2. Akshay Kumar
3. Nelson Mandela
4. Antarctica
5. No man's land
6. Archery
7. BANANA

Set 5

1. Wear it
2. Iris
3. Cricket
4. Kajol
5. Embassy
6. Tarot card
7. WICKET

MATHS AND IQ

1. TORTOISE
2. | 19 | Multiply | 3 | Plus | 14 | Minus | 67 | = | 4 |
3. ₹80
4. Manisha
5. | 38 | Minus | 14 | Plus | 21 | Divide | 5 | = | 9 |

VOCABULARY

1. NEON
2. MERIT
3. SAGE
4. WARD
5. DIVA

SPEED

1. Mouse
2. World War I
3. Yoghurt/Curd
4. He was the boy who was given the first vaccination against smallpox by Edward Jenner.
5. Yudhisthir
6. Serious
7. Two
8. Andhra Pradesh
9. Raj Kapoor
10. Painting

www.ingramcontent.com/pod-product-compliance
Lightning Source LLC
Chambersburg PA
CBHW030233170426
43201CB00006B/208